Proverbs 14:34, "Righteo

God's Cure
for our
Nation

Dr. James Wilkins

*"AMERICA, AMERICA, GOD SHED
HIS GRACE ON THEE..."*

Copyright © 2007
Dr. James Wilkins

PUBLISHED BY:

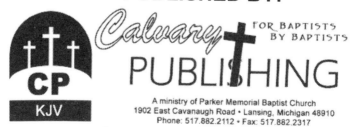

FOR BAPTISTS
BY BAPTISTS

Calvary PUBLISHING

CP
KJV

A ministry of Parker Memorial Baptist Church
1902 East Cavanaugh Road • Lansing, Michigan 48910
Phone: 517.882.2112 • Fax: 517.882.2317

w w w . c a l v a r y p u b l i s h i n g . o r g

Table of Contents

FORWARD

Anyone who knows anything about the Bible realizes that America is a very sick nation. The conflict of opinions is over how sick she is.

Some will say, "She is terminal; there is no hope."

Others are so busy living or doing their own thing they haven't even considered the question.

Many, may shrug their shoulders and say, this generation is no worse than previous generations. We just hear about it more.

GOD'S CURE FOR OUR NATION is a book which boldly attacks the defeatism and despair that grips the hearts of many of God's people and pastors who have all but given up hope for our country.

In **God's Cure for Our Nation** Dr. Wilkins pictures America as a seriously ill, even terminal patient, who seeks a doctor's opinion. The doctor examines the patient but defers his conclusion until other case histories of patients with similar symptoms can be analyzed.

The sickness of our apostate society is compared to **four other periods of extreme apostasies** found in God's sacred word.

The first case history is the rebellious Jews under the leadership of Moses who were placed in an isolation ward until many of that idolatrous generation died. The daily funerals and tears were good object lessons to the survivors as they buried their fathers and grandfathers who rebelled against God. Under the leadership of Joshua they crossed the Jordan into the Promised Land to great victories.

The second case history is the succession of apostasies which were only cured by a civil war that almost destroyed the tribe of Benjamin. The prophet Samuel followed by King David brought great glory and honor from the ashes of these **seven apostasies.**

The third case history, we find the Temple in shambles and Israel as a pagan nation having totally rejected the true God of heaven (except a remnant). There was no Bible preaching because the Bible (the Law of God) had been lost. Josiah, a boy of eight years old, whose father had been murdered, began the greatest reformation the world ever witnessed.

The final case history was the first apostasy **in the church era**. This period finds the great leader, Paul, in prison. He has been totally rejected by "all Asia" and at his trial, "no man stood with me". Because of this great rejection Paul was deeply depressed until he was comforted by God who equipped him to comfort Timothy and every pastor who will encounter a falling away from Bible Christianity. Paul leaves this world in victory having given Timothy reassurance and AN ANTIDOTE TO OVERCOME ANY PERIOD OF APOSTASY, INCLUDING OURS.

With the case histories proving that there is hope for America, Dr. Wilkins then turns his attention to the execution of the mandate which Jesus gave his church.

The mandate is **not soul-winning or teaching** the Bible, however, both of these elements are key ingredients to fulfilling His great commission to the church. The literal mandate in Matthew's account of the great commission is **"as ye go make men into disciples"**. The following verse reveals how well the church is to disciple its new converts. It is the same requirements that one finds in all other periods of spiritual awakenings. Disciple, literal the spiritual babies, well enough so they can disciple others.

There are three lessons on discipling new converts, which are contrary to the traditional practices found in the average church today. The emphasis is on protection and developing the new convert as soon as they are saved. A spiritual role model should be placed over each new convert in order to protect and develop him.

The spiritual therapy prescribed for the recovering patient is the same spiritual practices which God commanded in overcoming other dark days of apostasy. They are;

- ❖ **Powerful spirit filled preaching** by God's preachers
- ❖ **Periods of fasting and praying** by God's people
- ❖ **A rededication and a devoted effort honoring the Christian Sabbath** as a special day in worshiping God.

The final lesson makes an appeal for God's people to study and work as spiritual doctors in the Lord's nursery which will produce the quality of Christians that God will use to heal America.

This book basically is divided into three parts:

The refuting of defeatism which will **create new hope and faith in today's believers.**

The re-establishing of God's mandate and method to develop a vibrant base **in training spirit-filled, disciple-makers.**

The clear steps in the spiritual exercise which must be followed for the spiritual awakening. These steps will lead America back and will establish her again as a healthy, God fearing nation.

Dr. Wilkins believes that a terrorist attack or a series of terrorist attacks will be used by God to trigger a spiritual awakening **WHICH WILL CURE OUR NATION.**

NOTE: WHEN YOU SEE A (+) SIGN, IT INDICATES AN ANSWER TO A QUESTION IS BEFORE IT.

Grade yourself for best retention of subject matter.

A= Did the questions on Daily Basis

B= Did the questions before class time

J= Didn't complete lesson. "J" reminds one of the Judgment Seat.

FOR BETTER RETENTION OF MATERIAL

Read something one time and the average person can only recall 6% of what he reads two weeks later. But if one reviewed the key principles for 6 days his retention goes up on an average to 62%.

LESSON ONE
IS AMERICA TERMINAL?

This book will be divided into ten separate lessons. In our lesson we will use the allegory of a sick person who suspects that he is terminally ill.(+) He goes to a doctor who examines him and confirms his suspicions and pronounces him, "a very sick man". But before the doctor will pronounce him terminal, he states that he wants to study some case histories of others who had the same or similar symptoms.(+)

After the doctor studies other similar case histories he informs the patient that there is a slight chance that he can get well or at least postpone his imminent death IF – and ONLY IF – IF the person will strictly follow the prescribed therapy which the doctor outlines.(+)

THE EIGHT LESSONS IN THE ALLEGORY OF A SICK PERSON ARE:

- Is America Terminal?
- Reading the Inspired Charts of Other Patients
- Major Surgery without Anesthetic
- God's Antidote for Apostasy
- The Prevention Which Develops Good Health

- The Prescription and care which will lead to a healthy nation.
- Therapy which produces healing.
- Abundant health or destruction.
- Study and become a doctor.

THE PURPOSE OF THIS BOOK

The purpose of this book is to strengthen the faith of God's people in order for them to believe we can have a national spiritual awakening.(+)

First, The Bible declares that "...without faith it is impossible to please him [God]..." One must come to a point of faith before his works are acceptable to God and receive his blessings.(+)

GOD IS A PRESENT TENSE GOD

Second, the one coming to God must believe THAT HE (GOD) IS or is the great "I AM" or omnipresent God.(+) This means God is present everywhere and in answer to prayer can change the course of history.

Third, one must believe that this great "I AM" or present tense God will reward (answer his prayers and bless him) if he will diligently seek him. (Heb 11:5)(+)

Fourth, "...faith cometh by hearing and hearing by the word of God." (Rom 10:17)

Is America Terminal?

The first effort to strengthen God's people's faith is to examine some of the symptoms of our "patient". We will also reveal God's "x-rays" of another patient who had the same symptoms, but lived. Although the symptoms reveal that our nation has a deadly sickness; remember the old adage – **"where there is life, there is hope."**

The second effort to increase God's people's faith "so they can believe and have hope" is an examination of other case histories. These case histories reveal that **the patients were just as sick as our nation**, but they also revealed **some instructions** that help in their healing.

The third effort is to show the Biblical steps which lead to good health (+)

The fourth effort is to increase God's people's faith and bring back a healthy society by following **the prescribed therapy found in God's operational manual.(+)**

THE IDENTITY OF THE SICK PATIENT

As we study our lesson we find the identity of the sick patient is **not a person at all.** The sick patient is THE UNITED STATES OF AMERICA.

The stock market is robust and outwardly it seems like our nation is excelling, but a closer examination reveals a very different story.(+)

God's Cure for Our Nation

Would you say that the United States of America has become a sick society since the Bible, prayer and patriotism have been expelled from her schools?(+)

When one considers the widespread use of alcohol and drugs among her young people, the abandonment of the sanctity of marriage, and the decline of moral (Bible) values by the vast majority of her citizens, it is clear according to Bible standards, America has grave problems.

When one further considers the corrupt political leaders which embrace the one world philosophy and are dedicated in their efforts to destroy the foundation of Christian America, then it is clear we are in deep trouble.

The rapid growth of the Muslim and Mormon faiths also attests to our nations decline.(+) The acceptance of abortion and homosexual lifestyles are also indicators of our departure from God's healthy standards.

Lawlessness and gang activities make many inter-cities unsafe.(+) Even law enforcement do not patrol in these areas and our jails and prisons are overflowing with 2,000,000 inmates. The people of our country are deeply religious and practice a brand of Christianity, which is far below what the Bible teaches. This kind of Christianity which TEACHES THAT ONE IS A GOOD CHRISTIAN IF HE GOES TO

Is America Terminal?

THE CHURCH **OF HIS CHOICE** ONCE A WEEK HAS REPLACED THE BIBLE in defining what a new convert should do and how he should act after his conversion.

Would you agree that it is harder to develop a Spiritual baby who is born into such a sick society than it would be **if our nation were a godly nation?(+)**

THE SAME SLIPPERY SLOPES

The United States seems to be following England down the same slippery slopes to a godless society.(+)

England once was a Christian nation. Bibles published in England were sent all over the world. Their missionaries heralded the good news, that there is remission of sins through the shed blood of Jesus Christ. Their churches were healthy and evangelistic.

Now, England is an idolatrous and godless nation with only 3% of its citizens in church on any given week.(+) This includes the Catholics, Anglicans, Muslims as well as Christians.

According to a recent survey, the Southern Baptist Convention reported that 80% of all high school graduates here in the United States dropped out of church within a year or two after graduation from High School.(+)

DO THE MATH

The churches in rural America and in the small towns and villages, which used to be the backbone of Christian America, are dying.(+) All one has to do as he attends or visits different churches is to observe the average age of the people who are at that service. Counting the children and teenagers along with the adults the average age would probably average out to be around fifty years old.

At the rate of 80% lost of our teenagers each year, how long will it take until America joins England who has Ichabod (The glory has departed) written over the doors of its Churches?(+)

A DISTURBING QUESTION

Through the years, a disturbing question has been asked **"Where is America found in the Scriptures concerning Bible prophecy?"**(+)

Some people that your author considered "Doom Sayers" would answer "America is not found in Bible prophecy because she is not there; **she has been destroyed**."

They would point to the fact that there is no clear mention of the United States in Bible prophecy and to the way God has chastised Israel as their proof. It is obvious that God used other nations to chastise Israel when they went too far into idolatry and would not repent.(+) Then, these scholars would point to the Muslim nations, which have over a billion members, and are militant and support terrorists as America's destroyers.

Your author would always reject their arguments by saying, "America was not even discovered when the Bible was written. That's the reason it is not found in Bible Prophecy."

ONE REFERENCE OF THE UNITED STATES

Other scholars would say, "Yes, America is found in Bible prophecy, one time.(+) It is found in Ezekiel 38:13 which reads,"

> "Sheba, and Dedan, **and the merchants of Tar'shish, with <u>all the young lions</u> thereof**, shall say unto thee, Art thou come to take a spoil? hast thou gathered thy company to take a prey? to carry away silver and gold, to take away cattle and goods, to take a great spoil?"

They would explain that "the merchants of Tarshish" was England. The symbol of England is a lion and that the young lions represented the colonies which once belonged to England when she was a world power. They would point out that the young lions were the United States, Canada and Austria. If the interpretation of the young lions are correct, then this reference would fit America perfectly in today's world. This coming event is recorded in Ezekiel 38 and 39. THE RUSSIANS AND THE ARABIC NATIONS ATTACK ISRAEL. The role of England, America, Canada and Austria is **pictured as just "protesting" Russia's invasion of Israel**. These nations seemed to be using diplomatic channels to reason with this unprovoked attacked on Israel instead of helping to defend her. In your author's opinion, this would better describe America's role in Bible prophecy. As a sick nation with morally corrupt political leaders, **we no longer have the moral courage and will** to do much more than PROTEST.(+)

IN KEEPING WITH MAKING THIS WRITING A FAITH BUILDER

The good news for Israel is God will step in and miraculously stop Russia and the Muslim nations in their tracks. (Ezekiel 39:1-2) Five out of six of that huge invading army will be destroyed in a single day.(+)

Is America Terminal?

The bad news for America is we had better turn back to our **Operational Manual** and follow its principles in protecting and developing our spiritual babies or else we will reap the same judgment as Israel. The clock is ticking and time is running out.(+)

POINTS TO PONDER

- **America is a sick society because she has forsaken the Bible and the God of the Bible.**
- **God can heal her and make her strong once again**
- **II Chronicles 7:14 states the grounds for her healing**
- **I can pray and do my part in believing God and working toward a healthy nation.**

God's Cure for Our Nation

MONDAY
(The Identity of a Sick Patient)

1. We will use the _____ of a sick person who_____ he is_____ ill.

2. The Doctor wants to _____ some case_____ of others who had the_____ symptoms.

3. Only IF - _____ the person will_____ follow the _____ therapy.

4. The _____ of this book is to _____ God's people _____.

5. One must come to a _____ of faith before his_____ are_____ to God.

TUESDAY
(God is a Present Tense God)

1. The one _____ to God must believe that _____ (God)_____ or is the great _____ _____.

2. He must _____ that this great _____ _____ will reward if he _____ seek him.

Is America Terminal?

3. The old adage, "where there is_____, there is _____".

4. The Third _____ is to how the_____ steps which_____ to good _____.

5. An _____ of the _____ therapy found in God's_____ manual.

6.

WEDNESDAY
(The Identity of the Sick Patient)

1. Outwardly it seems like our _____ is excelling but a _____ examination reveals a different_____.

2. America has become a sick _____ since the_____, prayer and patriotism has been _____ from her schools.

3. The _____growth of the_____ and Mormons _____ attests to our nations_____.

4. Lawlessness and _____ activities make our _____ unsafe.

5. Would you _____ that it is _____ to develop a

_____ baby   who   is
_____ into such a sick society?

THURSDAY
(The Same Slippery Slopes)

1. The US seems to be _____
England down the _____ slippery
_____ to a _____ society.
2. England is a godless_____ with
only _____ of it citizens in
_____ on any given _____.
3. 80% of all high school _____
drop out of church within a _____ or
two after_____.
4. The_____ in rural America
which used to be the _____ of
Christian America are_____.
5. At the rate of _____ lost of our
_____   each   year
how_____   will   it   take
_____   to   join
_____?

FRIDAY
(A Disturbing Question)

1. Where is _____ found in the _____ concerning Bible _____?

2. It is obvious that God_____ other_____ to chastise.

3. We no longer have the _____courage to _____much more than_____.

4. Five out of _____of that_____ army will be destroyed in a _____ day.

5. The _____ is _____ and time is _____out.

MY COMMIMMENT

I will strive to keep an open mind concerning the possibility of a nation changing spiritual awakening and ask God for his mercy in sending it.

Name: _____

Daily Declaration

I will strive to believe God's Word and not the negative talkers of our day

Memory Verse

II Chronicles 7:14

"If my people, which are called by my name, shall humble themselves, and pray, and seek my face, and turn from their wicked ways; then will I hear from heaven, and will forgive their sin, and will heal their land."

	M	T	W	TH	F	S	S
AM							
PM							

LESSON TWO
CASE HISTORIES OF OTHER SICK SOCIETIES

The purpose of this book is to give God's people facts that will help their faith to grow.(+) In keeping with that purpose of making this writing a "Faith Builder" may we now turn our attention to other dark tragic periods of human depravity to look for hope and a cure for our nation?

We will examine the case histories from four different periods of time. The four case histories, which we will study are:

First, The case history of the patients whom God placed in isolation until the sickest patients died.(+)

Second, The case history of the patients who were only cured after the surgical procedure of a civil war.

Third, The case history of the sickest and darkest period of Israel's history where the patients could not be saved but obtained a better quality of life before dying.

Fourth, The case history of a heart breaking experience which brought life and hope to other sick societies.(+)

Before exploring these case histories may I give a word about the attending physicians?

The doctor of **case history one** was "doctor" Moses who died while operating on his patients.

The doctors in **case history two** are "doctors" Samuel and King David.

The doctor in **case history three** was "doctor" Josiah who began practicing medicine at the **tender age of eight**.(+)

The Doctor in **case history four is the heart specialist** and servant of the Lord, Paul, who prescribes a remedy of hope for our generation.(+)

GOD'S DESCRIPTION OF A
SICK SOCIETY

The true history of Christianity in the United States as well as the human race is one of high moral standards followed by a decline into putrid periods of apostasy.(+) Many people have the mistaken belief that just because America was established as a Christian nation, she has remained a nation of high moral principles until the last 50 years or so when she begin to decline into the backslidden nation that she is today. THIS IS NOT SO; history will not reveal that belief to be true.(+) There was a time or two in the past 300 years that America became so sinful she almost ceased to be a nation.(+) The same vices, which plague our society today, were dominate in the lives of those people also. Those vices, which can be found in all other periods of apostasy, including ours, were: (+)

- Drunkenness (drugs)
- Witchcraft
- Homosexuality (lust)
- Atheism
- Lawlessness
- A Spirit of defeatism (among Christians)

In fact, at one time in the United States, there were more books entitled **"The Age of Reason"** (on Atheism) than there were **Holy Bibles**.(+) Yet God sent the Great Awaking of 1734 that produced the greatest Christians America has ever seen. Since that time our country has experienced periods of spiritual awaking and revival followed by periods of decline, formal religion, rebellion and wickedness.

HOW GOD SEES A REBELLIOUS NATION

The words God used to describe a generation of religious Jews could be applied to many generations, including ours.(+)   He said:

> "Ah sinful nation, a people laden with iniquity, a seed of evildoers, children that are corrupters: they have forsaken the LORD, they have provoked the Holy One of Israel unto anger, they are gone away backward. Why should ye be stricken any more? ye will revolt more and more: **the whole head is sick, and the whole heart faint**.(+) **From the sole of the foot even unto the head** *there is* **no soundness in it**; *but* <u>wounds, and bruises, and putrifying sores</u>: they have not been closed, neither bound up, neither mollified with ointment." (Isaiah 1:4-6)(+)

The Book of Isaiah reveals how God dealt with and cleansed much of the corruption of Israel. He brought wars, famines and national calamites before that generation changed.(+)

Many believe that is what God is doing in America today, as she suffers from floods, fires, droughts, and storms and with the Muslim nations and terrorists waiting in the wings.

Let us see if our faith can began to have a little hope by examining **case number one**.

THE CASE HISTORY OF THE PATIENTS WHOM GOD PLACED IN ISOLATION UNTIL THE SICKEST DIED

There is much data found in the Bible that described the rebellion and idolatrous nature of the children of Israel. After the miraculous way God destroyed Egypt, Pharaoh and his army in the Red Sea; the Jews rebelled, complained and griped until God placed them in an "Isolation Ward" (wilderness) until the sickest ones died.

In the isolation ward for 40 years there were object lessons, which were amplified by many funerals and tears,(+) which taught the Jews what happened to sinful and rebellious people. God again, spoke to Israel through his attending physician and prophet Moses, who reminded the Jews that God had become angry with him because of their rebellion, so he would not lead them into the Promised Land. (Deut. 4:21) But it was time for them to go forward.

THE SAME ORDERS AND THE SAME REQUIREMENTS

The Jews soon learned that God had not changed his mind and the obedience that he required of their fathers and the command He first issued **were still just as much in effect as when He first issued them.**(+) Please examine the exact words of Moses as he re-issued the same commission to them as he did to their rebellious fathers: (+)

> "And Moses called all Israel, and said unto them, Hear, O Israel, the statutes and judgments **which I speak in your ears this day,** that ye may **learn them, and keep, and do them.**(+) The LORD our God made a covenant with us in Horeb. The LORD made not this covenant with our fathers, **but with us, *even* us, who *are* all of us here alive this day.**(+) The LORD talked with you face to face in the mount out of the midst of the fire, (I stood between the LORD and you at that time, to shew you the word of the LORD ..." - Deut. 5:1-5

Observe the strong, pointed words of Moses in Verse one-

"I speak in your ears"-   **Hear Them**

"That ye may learn them" – **Learn Them**

"Keep and do them" –   **DO THEM**

Observe the strong, pointed words of Moses in verses two and three:

God made a covenant with us; The Lord did not make this covenant with our fathers, **but with us, even us.** Please observe very closely the wording – NOT with our fathers (40 years ago) but with us, **even us.**

"Even us **who are alive this day"(+)**

Observe the strong pointed statement of Moses in verse four:

The Lord talked with you face to face. "The Lord talked with you face to face in the mount out of the midst of the fire." Moses is stating these words to them even though many of them were not there because of their age (over 35 years) He did this in order to emphasize the charge and responsibility given by God to Israel WAS AN IRREVOCABLE COMMAND.(+)

Observe the strong, pointed statement of Moses in verses five and six.

Moses is saying I stood before the Lord because you were fearful and you pleaded with me to act in your behalf. Verse six states I am the

God who saved you out of slavery and gave you freedom. With that freedom comes great responsibility and requirements.(+) Then in the following verses of that chapter God spells out what he expects of them.

In I Corinthians, the Bible declares that **NOW THESE THINGS** (referring to the experiences of the children of Israel) **WERE OUR EXAMPLES.** (I Cor. 10:6-11)

Study those verses and you will see that the commandments Moses gave the Jews as THEY WERE BEGINNING TO COME OUT OF A SICK SOCIETY were the same original commandments which God gave them years before.

Moses pointedly made that clear to them in order for us to receive the same pointed message in our day.(+) **They were examples unto us.** Our mandate found in Matthew 28:18-20 is still the churches marching orders today.(+)

The Jews after they came out of their isolation ward (wilderness) crossed over Jordan and had several years of victory and good health in their own land.

FAITH FACTOR

The faith factor for our generation is if God brought healing to that generation He is no respecter of persons and will heal our nation also if we will follow his instructions. **He will provide the leadership to bring health to our sick society if only we will accept our responsibility and follow.**

POINTS TO PONDER

❖ **God speaks to our ears and commands, HEAR THEM**

❖ **God speaks to our hearts and commands, LEARN THEM**

❖ **God speaks and commands, KEEP AND DO THEM**

❖ **Failing to do God's Words BRINGS APOSTASY**

❖ **Doing God's Word with all our hearts and with all of our Soul BRINGS REVIVAL**

❖ **THAT IS GOD'S POSITION AND HE WILL NOT CHANGE**

MONDAY
(Case Histories of Other Sick Societies)

1. The _____ of this book is to give_____ which will help their_____ to grow.
2. The_____ history of _____ placed in _____until the sickest died.
3. A_____ breaking experience which brought _____and _____ to other sick_____.
4. Doctor _____ began to_____ medicine at the_____ age of_____.
5. The _____ specialist,_____, who prescribed a remedy of hope for _____ generation.

TUESDAY
(God's Description of a Sick Society)

1. In the United _____as well as the_____ race is one of high_____ followed by a _____into apostasy.

Case Histories of Other Sick Societies

2.   This   is   not_____,   History
will_____   reveal
that_____ to be true.

3.   In the past_____ years America
became   so   _____she   almost
_____ to be a nation.

4.   Those   vices   which _____ be
found   in _____other   periods
of_____ including ours.

5.   The   age   of _____(on
atheism) than there was _____Bibles.

WEDNESDAY
(How God Sees a Rebellious Nation)

1.   God   described   a _____
of_____ Jews   could   be   applied
to_____   generations,
including_____.

2.   The _____head   is_____,
and the whole_____ faint.

3.   Wounds,   and _____,   and
putrefying_____;   they   have   not
_____, neither _____ up.

4.   He (God) brought_____, famines,
and_____ calamities before that
_____changed.

5.   In   the_____   ward
for_____   years   there

God's Cure for Our Nation

were_____ lessons amplified by
many _____ and
_____.

THURSDAY
(The Same Orders and the same Requirements)

1.   The_____ soon learned that
   _____ had not_____.
2.   Moses re-issued the
   _____commission to them as he
   _____ to their_____
   fathers.
3.   That ye may_____ them, and
   _____, and_____
   them.
4.   But_____ us, even_____,
   who are all of us here_____
   this_____.
5.   "Keep and _____ them"
   _____ them!

FRIDAY
(Observe the Strong Pointed Words in Verses 2 and 3)

1.   Even_____ who are
   _____ this_____.
2.   To emphasize the_____ and
   _____ given by God was an
   _____ command.

34

3. With that _____ comes great_____ and _____.

4. Moses _____ made that_____ to them in order for us to_____ the same _____message.

5. Matthew 28:18-20 is still the _____ marching _____today.

MY COMMIMMENT

I will strive **not to be** part of the problem but will work to become part of the solution in helping save our nation by obeying God's Word.

Name: _____

Daily Declaration

The Jews found that God's marching orders had not changed nor has our marching orders which are found in Matthew 28:18-20 changed.

Memory Verse

Hebrews 13:8

"Jesus Christ the same yesterday, and to day, and for ever."

	M	T	W	TH	F	S	S
AM							
PM							

- **GIVE YOURSELF AN "A"** if you filled in and reviewed the blanks on a daily basis. This will raise your potential of remembering on an average to 62%
- **GIVE YOURSELF A "B"** if you completed all your blanks before class time.
- **GIVE YOURSELF A "J" FOR JUDGMENT** in order to remind yourself that one has to give account of each day's activity when he takes his finals at the judgment seat of Christ
-

  MY GRADE FOR THIS WEEK IS____

NOTE: Fill in any blanks as you go through the key statement blanks if you have not done so.

LESSON THREE
MAJOR SURGERY WITHOUT ANESTHESIA

In this lesson we will deal with two case histories of other deep periods of apostasy. Each case history reveals that God brought much good from those dark periods which should give our generation hope and renewed faith.

THE CASE HISTORY OF THE PATIENTS WHO WERE ONLY CURED AFTER A SURGICAL PROCEDURE OF A CIVIL WAR

The book of Judges is a book that begins with great courage and spiritual leadership.(+) Joshua and Caleb lead the Israelites to great victories but they could not get their people **to be completely obedient to God's commands.** This compromise lead to further sins and soon Israel was in the first of **seven apostasies**.

GOD IN HIS MERCY INTERVENED

When things got so hopeless and the people could not stand the oppression of their sinful lives they called out to God (Judges 3:9). Each time the people **of the sin-sick societies** cried out, God always responded the same way, with a spokesman.(+)

GOD RAISED UP A SPOKESMAN WHO GAVE HIS MESSAGE

When one studies the different spokesmen God used in bringing revival it is clear that GOD IS MAKING A POINT, the point He is stressing is, one does not have to be brilliant or a profound preacher **in order to lead in a spiritual awakening;(+)** one just had to be willing to humble himself and do God's will.

GOD USED DIFFERENT SPOKESMEN

The message was always the same, THUS SAITH THE LORD or the spokesman demanded that the people obey God's Word.(+)

THE STRESS ON "DO THE WORD"

The strong statements which Moses, and then Joshua made concerning, "observe to do" is a constant effort of God to PREVENT APOSTASY AND PRESERVE A HEALTHY MORAL SOCIETY. In studying other case histories of apostasy and then a spiritual awakening which followed one will find this true. When they preached and practiced the principles of God's word they **enjoyed a period of God's blessings**.(+) But when they failed to do or failed to obey and do the word **things began to degenerate until they were in another deep apostasy.**

OUR PRESENT DAY APOSTASY

In order to explain how our present day apostasy began in America, may I take the liberty to explain a major contributing element? Some of the best people that I have ever known, along with people like myself contributed to sowing the seed **which grew into our modern day apostasy**. In doing so, I am not casting a reflection on personal soul-winning because at the age of 76 I still go out every Thursday night and Saturday morning. The people that I love and admire the most are people who are obedient to the command of the Bible to go.(+) The following testimony is only given to show that there is much more that we must do than go soul-winning, if we are to overcome our day of apostasy.

A PROBLEM CAUSED BY A
FAILURE TO OBEY

One of the primary reasons for the great confusion and rejection of organized religion in today's society is their disenchantment with "religion". The definition of being born again and being religious is **the same in the minds of our sick society.**

In the 1960 and 70's the general belief in America concerning becoming a Christian was basically accurate. The average person believed that;

- ❖ Becoming a Christian was the answer to all problems
- ❖ Becoming a Christian meant a changed life
- ❖ Becoming a Christian would make one happy

These beliefs are pretty well accurate if one follows the principles of the Bible AFTER BEING SAVED. But in that period of time the great commission as found in Matthew 28:18-20 was only used to admonish members to **give to missions**. This misinterpretation along with a heavy stress on soul winning brought **tens of thousands of people to churches** through the outreach programs and bus ministries.

Churches began to have junior church services to accommodate these large crowds. Since the bus ministry ministers to people from unstable families and in that day there were new "give-aways" almost every Sunday which caused a constant turn over in junior church. This constant turn over of new people burdened the heart of the junior church staff who believed that this may be the only time some of the poor kids will ever have a chance to be saved. A salvation message was preached every Sunday. Many, **many**, MANY PROFESSED to be saved. Hundreds more were saved in the outreach programs, but because of the masses of new people and the vivid awareness that people without Christ would suffer forever in hell another sermon would be proclaimed the following Sunday **on the good tiding that "Jesus Saves".**

There was absolutely no follow up on these thousands of new converts in most churches.(+) They were left in a hostile environment at the mercy of the devil and other religions.

Most of them became confused and disenchanted with organized religion.

To these disenchanted people religion had promised them **JOY**. Many times that JOY disappeared when they hit the front door of the dysfunctional home where they lived. Since they had no knowledge of what produces joy in a Christian's life they felt disappointed and let down.

Religion promised that "**getting saved**" would change them. It did for a little while but as **they continued to live in the world and to feed the fleshly nature, that change also disappeared** as the flesh began to dominate their lives once again.

Again, in their minds, RELIGION DIDN'T WORK; TO THEIR GREAT DISAPPOINTMENT.

As to their belief that becoming a Christian would solve all their problems, that too, didn't happen.

Many of these people **were so desperate in trying to change and find happiness** that they would be "SAVED AGAIN" AND "AGAIN" as they called it until they gave up and marked off "religion". In their disappointments they sank deeper into a life of no purpose nor hope. Living totally in the world with no spiritual intake the flesh begins to take over and grow. In many cases the flesh (people) grew to the level of addiction. This caused their lives to be void of any Christian values and caused many others to be turned away from God; lost forever.

WE ARE SUFFERING FROM THE WHOLESALE NEGLECT OF THAT GENERATIONS SPIRITUAL CHILDREN.(+)

It pains me to confess of my ignorance of the Bible in the earlier years of the ministry. As a pastor I did what I was taught to do. After a while when that didn't work I looked other places to find the answer in God's perfect Word. But the traditional way had blinded my eyes to the truth.

It also pains me to have to report that many of God's churches and preachers are still blindly following in the paths, which caused our apostasy. **The stress in the Bible is not soul winning!** The heart and soul of the bible is, AS YOU GO MAKE MEN INTO DISCIPLES. Our neglect to comprehend this truth led us to over stress soul winning. Overstressing soul winning without follow-up led to the environment where many, many, people in our sick society have no confidence in religion (churches).

TWO PRINCIPLES ALWAYS STAND OUT IN GOD'S WORD.

When the Bible or message of God was ignored – **apostasy would always follow.(+)** When the Bible was obeyed – a spiritual awakening would always follow.(+)

THE SEVENTH APOSTASY WAS THE WORST

Now, back to our case history. The statement found in the latter part of the book of Judges confirms the above statements.

"THERE WAS NO KING (ABSOLUTE) IN ISRAEL". The result was every man did what was right in his own eyes. Following the philosophy of no king (Bible as the Authority) in Israel and everyone doing what his conscience allowed him to do **was a springboard into the deepest and darkest of sin and corruption**. Judges chapter's 17 through 21 reveal the six prominent sins in every apostasy and the total breakdown of moral life in Israel.(+) This caused a civil war, and almost the total destruction of the Tribe of Benjamin in which at least 25,000 of their male population died.

The civil war seemed to bring Israel out of the wholesale acceptance of homosexuality, lewdness, idolatry and wickedness.(+) Under the prophet Samuel and then a shepherd boy, named David, whom God made king. Revival soon came again in Israel.

The darkest night that Israel ever experienced up to that time as a sin-sick people was FOLLOWED BY ISRAEL'S GREATEST PERIOD OF HOLINESS AND GLORY.(+)

LESSONS TO BE LEARNED WHICH WILL INCREASE OUR FAITH AND GIVE US HOPE FOR REVIVAL

First, a sick society is an ever-recurring problem as revealed in the Book of Judges.(+) There were seven periods of apostasies recorded in this one book.

Second, God will always heal when people began to adhere to and obey his word.

Third, After the darkest of nights (sick societies) **came the brightest of spiritual awakenings**.

Fourth, If God would use such a drastic surgical procedure that all the men of the Tribe of Benjamin except 600 were killed then he will do more than use **a few storms, droughts, 9/11 terrorist attacks before giving up on America.** People who know are waiting for the other shoe to fall…another terrorist attack in our beloved country is imminent.

BE SURE OF ONE THING, history teaches that God will take **drastic measures to save sinners from Hell!**(+) **And restore sick societies to good health.**

THE CASE HISTORY OF THE SICKEST AND DARKEST PERIOD OF ISRAEL'S HISTORY WHERE THE PATIENTS COULD NOT BE SAVED BUT OBTAINED A BETTER QUALITY OF LIFE BEFORE DYING

Our third case history reveals gruesome facts, which can be verified in the Book of II Kings (22 and 23) and in II Chronicles (34-36).

Israel had degenerated to the level that she did not EVEN RESEMBLE THE NATION that honored God and followed David in Israel's glory days.(+)

Because of the total abandonment of the Law of God and the embracing of the many false god's of her gentile neighbors, SHE WAS A PAGAN NATION.(+)

The three temples that Solomon had built to honor the false gods of three of his wives were flourishing (II Kings 23:13) while the house of the true God, which he had built, was in shambles (II Chronicles 35:8).(+)

The people of Israel were even allowing their children to be offered **by fire on the altar of Moloch.**(II Kings 23:10) (+)

Read the account of the idolatry and religion as recorded in the above chapters, which record the **lowest level of the moral life in Israel's history.**

In this sordid society the king was murdered. This brought to the throne **an eight-year-old boy**.

God had already pronounced doom and judgment on that generation. No one preached the Bible because no one had a Bible (God's Book of Laws). THE BIBLE HAD BEEN LOST and when they began to repair the house of God they found the **Word of God** (II Kings 22:8).(+)

THE GREATEST REFORMER WAS A KID

Josiah's dad was murdered when **he was eight years old** and he became king in a country where there were hundreds of religious services held each week in the temples of false gods but none in The House of God.(+)

Not only was there no Gospel preaching but there was no Bible. They had lost the Word of God.(+)

There is not a town or city in America as destitute of the truth as was Israel when Josiah began his brave crusade.

Josiah got saved and when **he was sixteen began to seek God with all of his heart and soul** (II Chronicles 34:3).

When Josiah **was 20 years old** he began to purge the land of all false idols and the revival was on.(+)

When He **was 26 years old** he begin to repair (build) the House of the God (II Chronicles 34:8).(+)

Shortly afterward they found the law of the Lord in the house of the Lord (II Chronicles 34:14) and began to read it. JOSIAH LEARNED OF THE IMPENDING DOOM of God's judgment from the Law of the Lord. (II Chronicles 34:24-25).

Josiah gathered all of the people before him and had the Law of the Lord read to the people and the spiritual awakening continued to grow. (II Chronicles 34:30)

Josiah made a covenant to keep the commandments **with all of his heart and with all of his soul, to perform the words of the covenant**, which was written in the book. (II Chronicles 34:32).

He continued to purge the land of false religions, and then he implemented the Passover supper and lifted every one in HIS SIN-SICK SOCIETY TO A BETTER QUALITY OF LIFE; but judgment still fell and the children of Israel were carried away in bondage. Daniel and the three Hebrew children were among those carried as slaves into Babylon which lead to the **spread of the Gospel through out the world.**

The greatest religious and political reformer of all time started the reformation of his day **when he was a teenager**. Perhaps this one fact will again stir the courage in young people like it did in the hearts of Daniel, Shadrach, Meshach and Abednego. The God who gave them courage and complete faith in Him **is the God who has always watched over America.**

LESSONS TO BE LEARNED WHICH WILL CAUSE FAITH TO GROW

- God is still God, even in the deepest periods of apostasy. **He can still give revival. (+)**

- God is still God and can use anyone, even a child, to do great things.
- God is still God and still blesses people **who love him with all of their heart, all of their soul and all of their might.**
- God is still God and will change a sick society if someone will only **obey and preach His Word.**

POINTS TO PONDER

❖ **The Bible has a consistent command to all generations of believers, "observe to do"**

❖ **The generation which is obedient is blessed of God**

❖ **The generations which do not "observe to do" are judged by God**

❖ **God's biggest complaint toward many generations is, "they say and do not"**

❖ **The hope of this generation is in obeying his command to "observe to do"**

God's Cure for Our Nation

MONDAY
(The Case History of the Surgical Procedure)

1. The book of Judges is a _____, which begins with_____ courage and spiritual_____.
2. Each _____ the people of the _____sick societies cried out, God always_____ the same way.
3. One does _____have to be _____ or a _____ preacher in order to lead a _____ awakening.
4. The _____ demanded that the _____ obey God's_____.
5. When they_____ and _____ God's work they_____ a period of God's _____.

TUESDAY
(Our Present day Apostasy)

1. People I _____ and_____ the most are obedient to the _____ of the Bible to_____.

Major Surgery Without Anesthesia

2. There was absolutely _____follow up on those_____ of new_____ in _____ churches.

3. We are_____ from the_____ neglect of that _____ spiritual children.

4. When the _____or _____ of God was_____ apostasy would _____ follow.

5. When the _____ was_____ a _____ awakening would follow.

WEDNESDAY
(The Seventh Apostasy was the Worst)

1. Judges chapter 17 through 21 _____ the_____ prominent sins in _____ apostasy.

2. The_____ war brought_____ out of the_____ acceptance of_____, _____, _____, and wickedness.

3. The darkest_____ was followed by _____ greatest period of_____ and_____.

4.   First, a sick _____is an
_____ _____ problem as
revealed in the _____ of Judges.

5.   Be   _____
of_____ thing, God will take
_____   measures   to
_____   sinners   from
_____.

THURSDAY
(A Case Study of a Sick Society that couldn't be Saved)

1.   Israel degenerated to a _____
that she did_____ resemble the
_____ that honored God in her
_____days.

2.   She embraced the_____ false
god's of her gentile neighbors, SHE WAS A
_____ NATION.

3.   The _____ Temples Solomon
had built to _____ the
_____god's of three of his
_____ were _____
while the _____ of God was in
_____.

4.   They were _____ allowing
their _____ to be offered by

Major Surgery Without Anesthesia

_____ on the _____
of _____.
5. When   he   began   to   _____   the
_____ of God they _____ the
Word of _____.

FRIDAY
(Let us Recount the Series of Events)

1.   Josiah's   _____   was
_____   when   he   was
_____ years old.
2.   There   was   _____   gospel
preaching   because   there   was
no_____.
3.   Josiah   was   _____   years   old
when he began to _____ the
_____ of all false idols.
4.   He was _____ years old when he
began   to   _____   the
_____ of God.
5.   God   is   still   _____, even in the
_____   periods   of
_____.   They   can
_____ give revival.

53

MY COMMIMMENT

I will strive to increase my faith by carefully studying God's word and by turning off all the negative cries of defeatism which is prominent in our society.

Name: _____

Daily Declaration

The God of Moses and Joshua is the great I AM. He helped them to overcome their deep apostasy and he will help us overcome ours also.

Memory Verse

Joshua 1:9

"Have not I commanded thee? Be strong and of a good courage; be not afraid, neither be thou dismayed: for the LORD thy God *is* with thee whithersoever thou goest."

	M	T	W	TH	F	S	S
AM							
PM							

- **GIVE YOURSELF AN "A"** if you filled in and reviewed the blanks on a daily basis. This will raise your potential of remembering on an average to 62%

- **GIVE YOURSELF A "B"** if you completed all your blanks before class time.
- **GIVE YOURSELF A "J" FOR JUDGMENT** in order to remind yourself that one has to give account of each day's activity when he takes his finals at the judgment seat of Christ

MY GRADE FOR THIS WEEK IS____
NOTE: Fill in any blanks as you go through the key statement blanks if you have not done so.

LESSON FOUR
GOD'S ANTIDOTE FOR APOSTASY

O ur final case history reveals the steps to overcome a period of apostasy. "Doctor" Paul, the apostle, is the physician in charge and he has written out a prescription to cure an apostasy.

THE CASE HISTORY OF A HEART BREAKING EXPERIENCE WHICH BROUGHT LIFE AND HOPE TO OTHER SICK SOCIETIES

The analysis of this case history has to be looked into with greater depth than the previous three case histories in order to give the reader **the faith to believe that God can heal our sick society.** The primary book that speaks of the details which reveals the hope and principles to overcome our sick society is in the second epistle which apostle Paul wrote to Timothy. Paul had two very important messages in his letter **to Timothy and to us.**

THE PURPOSE OF THE BOOK IS MISINTERPRETED

The book of second Timothy is not a book which warns of the terrible conditions **which will**

come upon a future generation in the far off "last days". The book of second Timothy is a book of instruction to a pastor on how to overcome the perilous last days which were confronting the churches of his day.(+)

Paul and Timothy and the other great leaders whose ministries are recorded in the book of Acts and in the epistles, were used to having great results which enabled the Christian to do marvelous works because of the fullness of the Spirit. **These same men were stunned and almost overcome when the first great falling away occurred.(+)**

The "last days" is not a period of time, which will begin in the last part of this dispensation. But the "last days" refers to the whole church or grace dispensation which started during the ministry of Jesus and the apostles.(+)

Hebrews 1:1-2 states God in times past spoke to past generations by the prophets but (notice the present tense verb), **"Hath these last days spoke unto us by his son."** How could Jesus have spoken unto them in the last days if the last days hadn't already begun?(+)

In Acts 2:15-21 is the recording of the prophecy found in Joel 2:28-32 and its fulfillment. Peter answered the question, "what meaneth this?" which was asked by those assembled on the day of Pentecost by quoting

Joel 2:28-32. He said (paraphrase) "what you are seeing right before your eyes is the fulfillment of a prophecy concerning the last days" (Acts 2:17).

How could it be happening in the last days if the last days wouldn't start for 2000 years? The proper teaching of when the last days started was during the ministries of Jesus and the Apostles. The "perilous days" recorded in II Timothy 3:1-5 are symptoms of the sick societies, which WOULD OCCUR, OVER AND OVER AGAIN IN FUTURE GENERATIONS.(+)

FROM SUCH TURN AWAY

"This know also, that in the last days perilous times shall come. For men shall be lovers of their own selves, covetous, boasters, proud, blasphemers, disobedient to parents, unthankful, unholy, Without natural affection, trucebreakers, false accusers, incontinent, fierce, despisers of those that are good, Traitors, heady, highminded, lovers of pleasures more than lovers of God; Having a form of godliness, but denying the power thereof: from such turn away." II Timothy 3:1-5(+)

Again, how could Timothy turn away from the perilous days, which would prevail in times of apostasy, if those perilous days were not happening in his day, right before his eyes?(+)

NOTICE THE OTHER PRESENT TENSE VERBS IN THE FOLLOWING VERSES

Present tense verb found in verse five – TURN (away)

Present Tense verbs found in verse six – ARE, (they) CREEP (into houses), And LEAD (captive)

Present tense verb found in verse seven – (ever) LEARNING

Present tense verbs found in verse eight – (so) DO (these) and RESIST (the Truth)

These present tense verbs indicate that those conditions were happening in Timothy's life, then.(+) These same "perilous times" would be repeated over and over again when God's people would become weak and stop preaching God's word with Holy Spirit power.(+)

Paul, the great apostle reminds Timothy of another falling away in Moses' day and told Timothy that the preachers who were compromising would get no further than those in the day of Moses did.(+) He even named the two men, Jannes and Jambres who rebelled against Moses just as he named the two compromising preachers Phygellus and Hermogenes, who opposed Timothy and himself. He then reassured

Timothy by saying, "But they **shall proceed no further**: for their folly shall be manifest unto all *men*, as theirs also was". (II Timothy 3:9)

NOTICE WHAT TIMOTHY
WAS INSTRUCTED TO DO

Paul instructed Timothy to remember that the life of a true preacher was one of dangers and trials (Verse 10-13). In verse 10 he reminded Timothy of his example of love and victorious service that Paul had set before him and the persecution which God had allowed him to overcome by enduring all the severe troubles and hardships. Paul was stating that THE "PERILOUS TIMES" WAS NOTHING NEW. Note, "but out of *them* all the Lord delivered me". (Verse 11) Paul's message to Timothy", God brought me through all those perilous times victoriously and HE WILL BRING YOU THROUGH victoriously also.(+)

THE LIFESTYLE OF A PREACHER
IN A DEEP APOSTASY

When all of the evils as described in verse one through five called "perilous times" come upon a generation **what reaction should the pastor have**?

HE IS TO CONTINUE ON IN THE FUNDAMENTALS OF THE FAITH, which he has been taught (verse 14)(+)

HE IS TO REMEMBER the firm biblical foundation he received and the lives of those who taught him. (verse 14-15)

HE IS TO REMEMBER THE INSPIRED SCRIPTURES which will completely equip him in all things (good works) (verse 16-17)

HE IS TO REALIZE THAT AMONG the good works which the Bible will fully instruct him is the instructions of how to overcome a period of falling away (Verses 16-17)

HE IS TO PREACH THE WORD (verse 2), which has been the constant command in all other periods of apostasy which brought revival and restored a healthy spiritual climate.(+)

HE IS TO FOLLOW GOD'S PLAN OF RECOVERY

If the Bible teaches that its purpose is to fully and completely equip God's people so they can do or perform every good work, then the Bible **must reveal the steps to overcome a period of apostasy.**

The simple outline of how to endure and then overcome a sick society is found in one verse. There are four steps which are found in II Timothy 4:5 and are so simply stated that we in **OUR TRADITIONAL MINDSET HAVE OVERLOOKED THEM.**

> "But watch thou in all things, endure afflictions, do the work of an evangelist, make full proof of thy ministry." II Timothy 4:5

Please note carefully some of the things which are included in those four simple commands.

First, Watch thou in all things

- Watch for his (Jesus) Second coming
- Watch your heart and don't become discouraged – A leader who demonstrates a spirit of discouragement cannot inspire others to follow. Quit all the negative talk about how hard it is or how hard your field of labor is. Negative talk sows unbelief in the lives of one's members and will make it harder to develop them in a walk of faith.
- Watch for the attacks of the devil. The devil loves to try and overwhelm a person when he is down or having troubles.
- Watch the members who are still true, especially the young converts; lest they are

drawn away by other groups. Remember, they are hurting also.

Second, Endure afflictions

- Losing members you love is heart breaking and it hurts. But it will strengthen and teach you how to walk by faith if you will let it (I Pet 5:10)
- Remember you are a soldier of Jesus Christ and endure hardness (II Tim 2:3).(+) Crying or complaining will not help anyone but will only make matters worse.
- God has promised to work all things together for your eternal good, if you will let him (Rom 8:28) Remember, you are an eternal being and he has your eternal welfare in mind.(+)

Third, Do the work of an evangelist

- The work of an evangelist **is winning souls.**
- The work of an evangelist **is preaching evangelically.**
- The work of an evangelist is TEACHING AND SHOWING people how to win souls in a classroom setting. Then, the soul-winner trainer (evangelist) **takes the trainees out and perfects them** in the vocation of winning souls by giving them

on-the-job-training from house to house until they too, **become trainers**. This brings new growth, joy and life back into the church.

- While you are in the process of doing the work of an evangelist remember building a solid foundation in the life of another takes time – endure afflictions still is commanded – **there is no quick fix** but you have a choice. You can just hold on or you can multiply. Multiplying means developing new members. The process of developing new members is slow and takes time. So you have to remember the command, and endure afflictions.

Fourth, make full proof of thy ministry

- This making full proof of thy ministry means to incorporate the principle of protecting the new converts from the sick society, while you are building a new army of disciples. You must place a role model over each member as you develop a new army. The new army will begin to multiply and start the process of carrying the gospel to every creature in the world. (We are still under God's mandate to do so)
- Careful reading and following of the principles of discipleship found in our

CHURCH'S OPERATIONAL MANUAL will work.(+) It has worked in the past and it will work in our sick society, IF WE WILL WORK IT! In the following lessons are many Biblical principles, which will aid in making full proof of thy ministry.

TO HELP TIMOTHY TO GET OVER HIS HEARTBREAK

We will now turn our attention to the other main reason that Paul wrote the second epistle to Timothy. Timothy was **suffering under deep bereavement and depression.** Things seemed to be falling apart all around him and the dearest person in the world, his spiritual father, **was scheduled to be executed**.

One of the main reasons Paul was writing to Timothy was to help him get over **the heartbreak of their defeat in Asia**.(+) Both Paul and Timothy were in Asia (Acts 20:4) where tens of thousands of people were saved. Many churches had been started and every person in Asia had heard the Word, both Jew and Greek (Acts 19:10)

Two wicked compromising preachers Phygellus and Hermogenes had successfully turned every one of their converts away from following the Bible (II Tim 1:15)

This terrible defeat and heartbreak had caused Paul as much or more pain than it did Timothy. In fact it had thrown Paul into **a state of depression that for a period he didn't even want to live**.(+) This statement is so out of harmony with the image people have of the great apostle Paul that one cannot believe it unless he hears it from Paul, himself. In II Corinthians we have his words: "For we would not, brethren, have you ignorant of our trouble which came to us in Asia, that we were pressed out of measure, above strength, insomuch that we despaired even of life:"(+)

Note where the trouble, which caused Paul such pain, came from! It came from ASIA.(+) Notice his description of his mental and physical condition.

Pressed out of measure - completely depressed

Above strength – beyond our endurance

Insomuch we despaired even of life – didn't think he would live through it – almost to the point that he didn't know if he wanted to live through it.

WHY WAS PAUL SO DEPRESSED?

Why was Paul, who could face any trouble; beatings, angry mobs, or even death in a victorious way, thrown into deep depression? Why was Paul so grieved and heartbroken?

He knew that the ministry that he and the others who went with him into Asia and established churches which would continue to reach others, disciple them and have a world vision to reach the lost world HAD BEEN CRIPPLED.

He also knew the type of ministry, which the compromising preachers, Phygellus and Hermogenes had. It was a ministry, which would serve the needs of the members and not stress the mandate which Jesus gave to the first church, **as you go make men into disciples**. These two preachers were men who would "tell the people what they wanted to hear (tickle their ears) instead of challenging their members to give their lives to God in an effort to save people from hell.

Paul knew that within a few years the good healthy spiritual conditions of Asia would become like the condition of the people in Josiah's day.(+) The compromise of Phygellus and Hermogenes would grow and produce the same results that Solomon's did while the truth that Solomon preached died. Solomon's compromises grew and destroyed all the good that he did in his early ministry.(+)

Paul wept because he knew the compromise of the two preachers would turn Asia back into a dark religious wilderness with no Gospel light within a few years. Coming generations would die lost. The reality of the masses going to hell because preachers of one generation compromise the Bible in **order to be popular and have a big church** grieved Paul to the point of depression. History bore out Paul's great concern. Most of Asia have suffered because of the ministry of these two compromising preachers, for the past 2,000 years.(+)

ALL THINGS WORK TOGETHER FOR GOOD

Paul wanted to have fellowship with the suffering Christ. He prayed for it (Phil. 3:10). One of the sufferings of Christ was total rejection and abandonment. God sent that type of pain and suffering unto the soul of Paul through the rejection and abandonment of those in Asia. At first Paul did not realize what his depression and pain was all about but God made him remember the prayer he prayed desiring fellowship with Christ's suffering. When Paul realized God was answering his prayer it made Paul happy and he began to rejoice.

Paul also prayed that he would be made conformable to the death of Jesus (Phil 3:10). Jesus died on the Cross-while Paul died as a martyr on the chopping block. Paul realized that another prayer had been answered and rejoiced.

PAUL'S FINAL GREAT
WORK FOR CHRIST

When Paul was crushed and suffering so much agony because of the great falling way of the churches in Asia **God comforted him.**

God saw all the future dark days of apostasy, which would break so many of his servant's heart. He sent his servant, Paul, through such pain in order to teach him how TO COMFORT ALL OTHER PASTORS WHO WOULD EXPERIENCE A "FALLING AWAY".

Again listen to the apostle Paul in his own word as he confirms this point:

"Blessed *be* God, even the Father of our Lord Jesus Christ, the Father of mercies, and the God of all comfort; Who comforteth us in all our tribulation, **that we may be able to comfort them which are in any trouble**, by the comfort wherewith we ourselves are comforted." II Cor. 1:3-4 (+)

God's Cure for Our Nation

When Paul was finally healed by his heavenly father and comforted he could comfort Timothy and future pastors, He wrote his final letter to his son in the ministry and basically told Timothy:

- I know and understand your tears, but through this letter you can see I am not abandoned and lonely. I'm dying as a victorious champion.
- My greatest desire was to have fellowship with my Lord in his suffering and be conformed to his death. Those prayers have been answered.
- I look forward to my graduation from the earth and my home going.
- This letter will help you to get your eyes back on your purpose and ministry.
- You will overcome your "perilous times" just like Moses and men of other sick societies have before you.
- My graduation day in which I will depart from this earth and receive his "well done" is immanent.

I leave with you and to every other pastor a RECIPE TO OVERCOME ANY DARK DAY OF APOSTASY.(+) It is not new and its principles have been followed many times **to**

restore sick societies back to good health.
Remember son, the four simple steps to good
health are;

1. **Watch in all things**
2. **Endure affliction**
3. **Do the work of an evangelist**
4. **Make full proof of the ministry**

The principles in the fourth case history
which will cause the people of this age to
believe and have greater faith are:

First, The world has experienced many
recurring periods of sick societies.

Second, God loves people and wants to
heal them of their rebellion and sin.

Third, compromise always brings God's
judgment.

Fourth, God always honors and blesses
people when they obey and teach God's
"word".

Fifth, God gave four absolutes steps to a
healthy society.

Sixth, If God overcame the sin of sick
societies of the past, he will bless and use us
to bring healing to our nation today…IF…

…IF…

IF WE WILL turn to his Operational Manual and follow the steps in raising good healthy babies into strong, healthy Christians.

POINTS TO PONDER

- **Paul's heart was broken when the first apostasy in the Christian era destroyed his greatest work.**
- **God comforted Paul so he could comfort others who would experience the same pain.**
- **Paul comforted Timothy by reminding him of the apostasy in Moses day.**
- **If God gave Moses victory over apostasy then God would give Timothy victory over apostasy.**
- **Then God gave Timothy the principles to overcome apostasy**
  1. **Watch in all things**
  2. **Endure afflictions**
  3. **Do the work of an evangelist**
  4. **Make full proof of the ministry**

God gave hope for a great Spiritual awakening in our day.

MONDAY
(A Recipe of Victory)

1. Second Timothy instructs pastors on _____ to _____ the _____ last days which is confronting them in their day.

2. These men were _____ and almost _____ when the great falling away_____.

3. The _____ days refer to the _____ grace or church_____.

4. How could _____ have spoken in the _____ days if the _____ day hadn't already _____.

5. II Timothy 3:1-5 are _____ which will occur _____ and _____again in future generations.

TUESDAY
(From Such Turn Away)

1. But _____ the _____ thereof from_____ turn _____.

God's Cure for Our Nation

2. How could Timothy _____ away from times if they were _____ happening?

3. These _____ tense verbs indicated that those _____ were _____ in Timothy's day.

4. Perilous days would come when God's _____ would stop_____ God's word with Holy Ghost power.

5. Paul reminded Timothy of _____ falling away in _____ days.

WEDNESDAY
(Notice What Timothy Was Instructed To Do

1. Paul _____ to Timothy was, he brought me through_____ and he will _____ you through.

2. He is to _____ on in the fundamentals of the_____ which he had been_____.

3. Preach the Word has been a _____ command in all_____ periods of _____ which brought_____.

4.   Remember you are a _____ of _____ Christ and _____ hardness.

5.   Remember, you are an _____ being and he has your _____ good in mind.

THURSDAY
(Do The Work of an Evangelist)

1.   Following   of   the_____ of_____   found in our Church's _____   manual will_____.

2.   Paul   was   writing   Timothy   to _____   him   get _____his _____ of their _____ in Asia.

3.   For a _____ Paul didn't even want to_____.

4.   We   were   _____   out of_____,   above_____, insomuch we _____.even of life.

5.   Note where the _____, which caused Paul such pain came from! It_____ from_____.

FRIDAY
(Why was Paul so Depressed?)

1. Paul knew the healthy_____
    conditions of Asia would _____like
    the_____   in   Josiah's
    _____.

2. Solomon_____   grew   and
    _____ all the good that he
    _____ in his _____
    ministry.

3. Most   of   _____
    have_____ because of the
    ministry of these two_____
    preachers, for the past_____
    years.

4. That   we   may   be   able   to
    _____ them which are in
    any_____.

5. I _____ with you and to
    every_____   a
    _____ to overcome any dark
    day of_____.

Daily Declaration

I will strive to be part of the solution of our apostasy by observing to do, instead of being part of the problem.

MY COMMIMMENT

I will strive to be part of the antidote for our apostasy by following Paul's inspired instructions.

Name: _____

Memory Verse

II Timothy 4:5

"But watch thou in all things, endure afflictions, do the work of an evangelist, make full proof of thy ministry."

	M	T	W	TH	F	S	S
AM							
PM							

LESSON FIVE
PROBLEMS TO BE SOLVED IN ORDER TO OBTAIN GOOD HEALTH

Before a medical doctor can prescribe a solution that will bring about healing to the patient, he must have a thorough understanding of the patient's condition. This is just as true when the patient is a nation and God has already emphatically declared, "The wicked shall be turned into hell, **_and_ all the nations that forget God**." Psalm 9:17

FUZZY THINKING ABOUT THE PROBLEM

A person may say "What is the problem? I know we have one but what is it?" Another person may say, "I don't have the answer, in fact, I don't even know the question."(+) These statements illustrate the general thinking of most leaders today concerning the major apostasy which grips society.

THE PROBLEM EXPOSED

America is a backslidden nation who has turned her back on God. Our society is dominated by false religion, hypocrites, atheism, and compromising believers. Our local churches are filled with careless and nominal believers.

THE CAUSES EXPOSED

There are **three main reasons** why our country is so backslidden, our society so putrid, and our churches so weak and powerless.

1. **The Poor, Careless Practice of Nominal Believers**
   - ❖ Our churches are filled with careless, nominal believers.(+)
   - ❖ The effect of the nominal believer's life is the primary cause for **the loss of new converts**.
   - ❖ The loss of new converts has a **shattering effect** upon some and a **discouraging effect upon all.**(+)
   - ❖ The effects of the new convert going back to his old life **turns many lost people away** from Christ forever.
   - ❖ This vicious cycle can only get worse as the conditions in the churches and in society continue to deteriorate as **they forsake the Bible. But there can be a change.**

2. **The Horrible Example of Those in the Religious, Political, Sports, and**

Entertainment World Causes the Average Citizen to Exclaim, "What's the Use?"

This has a shattering effect upon everyone because people learn more by observation than any other form of teaching. Disenchantment wounds and breeds discouragement and apathy.

3. **The Wrong Method of Feeding and Developing the Flock!**

   ❖ The third cause for our apostate condition reflects directly to the failure of the average local church and pastor.

   ❖ Pastors attempt to feed their flocks **from the pulpit** or classroom.(+)

   ❖ They attempt to feed as they teach or preach Bible messages.

   ❖ They preach or teach Bible messages, which have good content, are presented in a good way, and attain their goal of **clarifying the word.**

   These messages, if followed, hit the goal of clarifying the Word, **but miss the Biblical requirement completely.**(+) We are to do more than "**Teach the Word**" we are to teach people **how to "Do the Word".** When we just analyze the Bible, **we make Christianity a philosophy.** When we obey what Jesus commanded, **"Teaching them to observe** (or do) **all things ...**" we teach people to become disciples or practicing Christians. The stress in the Bible is for the Christian **TO DO OR OBSERVE THE WORD**, not just believe or understand its teaching.

In this lesson we will present two principles that God placed in the Bible, which, if followed, will correct this apostate condition. These principles deal with the method of teaching or training.

PROBLEMS CAUSED BY A FAILURE TO OBEY:

WE MUST BECOME AWARE OF THE PROBLEMS

Most of the older people in our churches, including the pastors, cannot grasp the solution to solve the problems in our spiritually sick society. Please consider a couple of the reasons why they have a hard time **grasping the solutions** to the problems, which are destroying our nation.

First, their own personal experience after they were saved greatly hinders their understanding.(+)

They reason, "No one had to FOLLOW UP ON ME when I got saved. I wanted to be baptized and start working for the Lord." They continue to reason, "If people really got saved they, wouldn't need anyone to follow up on them."

For those who have that testimony, please examine **the time and spiritual background (home) you came from**. In all likelihood, it was from an era of America that was still Christian in nature. By that, I mean people of your community or family understood what the Bible taught as well as what was expected of the person who got saved. **They were expected to live a changed life, be baptized, and join the church.** Therefore, once you were saved, it was natural for you to join the church and begin living a Christian life.

People of this day DO NOT have that understanding. Often it is just the opposite. Today the lifestyle of the Christian and non-Christian, in many cases, **are about identical**. The new convert doesn't know what is really expected of him because **he has been raised in a non-Christian society**.(+)

The way a new convert learns is from observation of others. Often the examples that he observes in our sick society are careless and many are unfaithful in their church attendance.

ANOTHER REASON IT IS HARD for some of our older members to grasp the biblical method of raising spiritual babes is because **they were not raised that way.** There was VERY LITTLE

OR NO FOLLOW UP AND PROTECTION of the young converts done in their churches.(+) It became easier for some to mark the new convert who dropped out of church **AS A LOST PERSON** and continue on in their traditional church life rather than try to find a solution in the Bible that would prevent the new convert from being lost from Christian service.

WE MUST BECOME KEENLY AWARE OF OUR SICK SOCIETY

Anyone who is realistic will acknowledge that **we are in a very religious but sick society**. Many of the people who are saved today **are at ground zero** as far as having any Bible knowledge. Much of the time the things they think they know are not scriptural. WE MUST RECOGNIZE THE TIME WE ARE IN AND BEGIN TO FOLLOW THE BIBLICAL PATTERN IN DEVELOPING OUR NEW CONVERTS.(+)

WE MUST BEGIN TO RESPOND TO A PERSON WHO RECEIVES CHRIST AS A BABE IN CHRIST

- He is not a number, prospect or statistic. He is a living, spiritual baby.(+)
- He is not just a blessing to be thankful for one minute and then rush on to our next

event. He is the newest member of God's family AND IS YOUR BABY BROTHER.

- He is a new member of God's family who will **either become a blessing or a liability.**

A BLESSING

If he is protected and developed, many more people will be led to the Lord because of his life and testimony.(+) A happy, contented baby who grows into a fruitful, dedicated member will be **the cause of many being saved**.

In his changed life and joyful testimony, the church has someone who **has credibility with all of his family, co-workers, and friends**. They now become people who are **very open** to the Gospel. Although Isaiah 60:22 is referring to those saved in the millennium, it could also describe the potential of one new convert who is fully surrendered to be used of God; ("A little one shall become a thousand, and a small one a strong nation: I the LORD will hasten it in his time.")

A LIABILITY

If the new convert (baby) is not protected and developed, he will soon drop back into his old lifestyle.(+)

The reason he is being overcome and confused is HE NOW HAS TWO NATURES, the spirit and the flesh.(+) When he is home **he still feeds the flesh** by watching television. At work or in school **he still feeds the flesh.** The conversation around him, the dress, the acceptance of permissive sex and worldly amusements are what goes into his mind all day long, and **it feeds the flesh.** Many do not respect the fact that he has become a Christian and is trying to live the Christian life. In fact, it is just the opposite with **some who are attempting to draw him back** into his past lifestyle.

The same attack that destroyed Lot's Christian life (seeing and hearing… II Peter 2:8) will also destroy your little baby brother if you allow it. **AT THE WORST,** he will go back to his old lifestyle confused and disenchanted with Bible Christianity. **AT THE BEST**, he will become a nominal Christian, which is exactly what the devil wants. Either way HE WILL BECOME THE SOURCE OF WORRY AND PAIN TO THOSE WHO WON HIM TO CHRIST; a hindrance to the cause of Christ instead of a blessing. HIS FAILURE WAS INSURED by the neglect he received when he came into God's family as a little baby.(+)

Just as Isaiah 60:22 refers to the thousands that will be saved by the life of one person, the same effect is true concerning the misspent life of a confused backslidden Christian, many will observe his poor testimony and turn away from Christ and never be saved.

Lot, a backslider, while in a drunken stupor, fathered a baby by the name of Moab. Hundreds of years later God had to destroy Moab who had grown into a large nation.(+) The boy fathered by a drunken backslidden father and a lost ungodly mother grew up and embraced pagan religion which caused tens of thousands to go to hell. This should cause every Christian to think and dedicate his life to Christ. Read the account of his destruction in Isaiah 15:1-9.

We need to learn to look at a baby Christian in the light of eternity and realize what he will become in future generations. We must not just push him aside **because of our busy schedule**.

BECOME AWARE OF THE POSSIBILITY OF CHILD ABUSE

Some of the most tragic stories one reads about in the newspapers **are stories of child abuse**.(+) Mothers and, most of the time, live-in boy friends do horrible things to poor innocent little children. One wonders what the newspapers, if there are any in heaven, would be reporting about the neglect that newborn babies **are**

receiving in many churches today? Instead of love and protection from the onslaught and deception of the world and the devil **they are all but abandoned to make it on their own**. There is no daily newspaper following the tragedy of neglect or abuse, but **be assured that a record is being kept, which people will have to face at the judgment seat of Christ.**

DEFINITION OF CHILD ABUSE

"The mistreatment of an infant or child either intentional or non-intentional which brings physical or mental pain and harm.(+) This is not the legal definition of child abuse but it is close enough to make the point.

Most of God's pastors and people **would not willfully harm one of God's little ones**. In fact, Jesus gave a grave warning of severe judgment to those who offended or abused a child. He states the warning in Matthew, Mark and again in Luke 17:2. NOTE the severity of his warning

"It were better for him that a millstone were hanged about his neck, and he cast into the sea, than that he should

offend one of these little
ones."

A DIRECT CHARGE TO THE PASTOR

When Jesus gave the **pastoral charge to the first pastor** he was very pointed in his words, "FEED MY LAMBS." By commissioning the pastor to feed (literally pacify) my lambs, or babies, Jesus left very little room for misinterpretation.(+)

Paul, as the example to all pastors and Christian workers, described himself **as a nurse who tenderly cared for his spiritual babies.**(+) (I Thessalonians 2:7). He further described how he developed the growing children who were under his pastoral care. In verse 10 **he describes himself as a role model** (behaved himself in a holy and unblameable way) and **as a father** who exhorted, comforted (encouraged), and charged them in their Christian life.

A DIRECT CHARGE TO THE MEMBERS

The use of the plural nouns "WE" and "OUR" in the testimony of Paul indicates that he had others helping him protect and develop his spiritual babies. The great commission, "**as ye go, make men into disciples**", places the care and development of new converts upon each member of the church family. The direct charge of Paul to:

"… let each esteem other better than themselves … Look not every man on his own things, but every man also on the things of others." (Philippians 2:3,4) shows the responsibility placed on each believer.

We need to take careful note of the responsibility that GOD'S OPERATIONAL MANUAL places upon each of us believers if we want to escape the **charge of child neglect or worse—child abuse** at the judgment seat.

Ignorance of the law is not an effective defense in a court of law.(+) God will judge each of us according to the principles found in HIS OPERATIONAL MANUAL. **It is our business as his children to learn and then conform to its teaching.**

THE SPIRITUAL INDUCING OF LABOR

Let us apply another physical practice to raising spiritual babies.

THE HARDSHIP AND DANGERS OF INDUCING LABOR

There may come a time when the welfare of the mother, or the child she is carrying, becomes endangered. In order to protect one or both of their lives, the doctor performs a procedure, which is called **inducing labor**. The dangers of performing such a procedure or not performing the procedure are carefully weighed and a decision is made.

A doctor performs tests and takes careful thought before he even considers inducing labor.(+) He knows that a baby who is a "premie", or one who is not allowed to stay in the womb and develop naturally for the full term of nine months, runs the risk of severe difficulties or even death.

Likewise, in the spiritual realm we have many who rush in, give the basic principles of the Gospel, which causes one to be born into God's family. MANY OF THESE "PREMIES" ARE LEFT WITHOUT PROPER HELP AND WILL NEVER DEVELOP INTO HEALTHY CHRISTIANS.(+)

NO MOTIVATION TO CHANGE

Consider the situation of a spiritual "premie". He generally belongs to a religion, **which rules their members by fear**. These religious institutions teach that if you are not a member of our church and don't keep our teachings to the end, **you will go to hell.** The premie has been convinced of that teaching, but he **feels empty and inwardly believes and longs for something** that will calm his fears and give him peace. His whole family is involved in that same belief system, and **he is extremely loyal to his family and church.**

Along comes a soul-winner that engages in a spiritual conversation with the concerned person.

The person becomes convinced of something that HE ALREADY KNOWS—I am a sinner. He also becomes convinced of something HE ALREADY FEARS—I am going to hell. This causes him a real problem. He can see himself as a lost sinner who is going to hell.

Then the soul-winner PROCEEDS TO SOLVE THE PROBLEM for him by showing him that Christ died as his substitute on the cross to save him from hell.

He becomes convinced of the truth of the Gospel and calls upon the name of the Lord. HE IS SAVED FROM HELL. He has peace and his fear is gone. **The message of the Gospel induces labor and he comes into God's family as a PREMIE.(+)** At this point he only knows that he called upon the name of the Lord, and doesn't yet suspect that there is anything else that he should do.

Many times the soul-winner **rushes on** without leaving any instruction for the new convert. The soul winner makes no further plans for following up on the new baby. **The new convert is in his religion**, he is still loyal to his family, but now **the motivation to make a change is gone.**

Although he has been wonderfully born into God's family, he still is controlled **by his family and the fear he has of breaking with the church**. He is a little baby without proper instruction or help. Judging by the definition of the world's standard he is all right **because he goes to the church of his choice each Sunday.(+)**

NO KNOWLEDGE THAT HE IS SUPPOSED TO CHANGE

One can lead a person who is dead in trespasses and sin, with no spiritual illumination, **to a new birth experience in a period of thirty minutes to an hour.** But during that time frame, nothing is said about the changes in the lifestyle of the new believer or any Christian responsibilities, which the new convert should make.(+)

The soul-winner has been programmed to win a soul and then joyfully report, "We got one tonight!" as if reporting a sale. Most of the time he has no sense of responsibility to the baby he just helped to bring into the world.

With no instructions and with a deep loyalty to family and church it is no wonder that the baby doesn't show up at the "new church" the following Sunday.

Later, when the effort is made to get the new discipled and into church, one is met with coldness and avoidance.

In our modern day, sick, religious society he has observed that it is acceptable for him to **go to the church of his choice one time a week.** He resists any effort to change his now, **comfortable lifestyle.**

As the apostle Paul stated, "But covet earnestly the best gifts: and yet **shew I unto you a more excellent way**." (I Corinthians 12:31)

In the next chapter we will attempt to give some principles which can lead to the healing of our nation.

POINTS TO PONDER

- ❖ **Failure to give proper instructions at his birth contributes to our apostasy.**
- ❖ **Failure to warn the baby of impending dangers contributes to our apostasy.**
- ❖ **Failure in using the right method in feeding the new convert contributes to apostasy.**

- ❖ **Failure to appoint a role model over the new convert adds to apostasy.**

Problems to be Solved

MONDAY
(Fuzzy Thinking About the Problem)

1. I don't have the _____, in fact, I don't even know the _____.
2. Our _____ are filled with _____, nominal_____.
3. The _____ of new converts has a shattering _____upon_____ and discouraging effect upon _____.
4. Pastors_____ to _____ their flocks from the _____ or _____.
5. These_____, if followed, hit the goal of _____ the Word, but _____the biblical _____ completely.

TUESDAY
(Problems Caused by the Failure to Obey)

1. Their own _____ experience after they were_____greatly _____their under-standing.
2. The new convert _____ know what is expected of him because he has been _____ in a non-Christian _____.

3. There was very _____ or no
    _____up   and
    _____done in their churches.

4. We must _____ the time we are in
    and_____to   follow   the   Biblical
    _____ in developing our new converts.

5. He is _____ a number, _____ or
    statistic. He is a _____, spiritual
    baby.

WEDNESDAY
(A Blessing)

1. If   he   is   _____
    and_____many
    more_____ will be led to the Lord
    because   of   his_____   and
    _____.

2. If a new convert (_____) is
    _____ protected and developed he will
    _____ drop back into his _____
    lifestyle.

3. The   reason   he   is   being
    _____and
    _____ is he now has two
    _____, the _____
    and the _____.

4. His   _____was
    _____ by the _____

he received when he came into God's family as a little _____.

5. Hundreds of _____ later God had to _____ Moab who had _____ into a_____ _____.

THURSDAY
(Become Aware of the Possibility of Child Abuse)

1. Some of the most _____ stories one reads in the _____ are the stories of _____ abuse.

2. The _____ of an _____ or a child either intentional or _____ which brings _____ or mental pain and _____.

3. By _____ the pastor to _____ my lambs (literally _____) my lambs, or babies, Jesus left very little _____ for _____.

4. Paul, as an _____ to pastors, described him-self as a _____.

5. Ignorance of the _____ is not an _____ defense in a _____ of law.

FRIDAY
(The Spiritual Inducing of Labou)

1.   A _____ performs tests and takes careful _____ before he _____ inducing labor.

2.   Many of these "_____" are left without proper help and will ____ develop into _____ Christians.

3.   The _____ of the Gospel _____ labor and he comes into God's family as a _____.

4.   Judging by the _____ of the world's _____ he is _____ because he goes to the church of _____ choice on Sunday.

5.   Nothing is said about the _____ in the lifestyle of the new believer or any Christian _____, which the new convert_____ make.

Daily Declaration

I will strive to look upon every new convert as my baby brother/sister and help them to become established as a Christian.

Problems to be Solved

MY COMMIMMENT

l will work at becoming more aware of our spiritual babies and how I can protect and develop them.

Name: _____

Memory Verse
Galatians 5:13

"For, brethren, ye have been called unto liberty; only *use* not liberty for an occasion to the flesh, **but by love serve one another.**"

	M	T	W	TH	F	S	S
AM							
PM							

- **GIVE YOURSELF AN "A"** if you filled in and reviewed the blanks on a daily basis. This will raise your potential of remembering on an average to 62%
- **GIVE YOURSELF A "B"** if you completed all your blanks before class time.
- **GIVE YOURSELF A "J" FOR JUDGMENT** in order to remind yourself that one has to give account of each day's activity when he takes his finals at the judgment seat of Christ
-

MY GRADE FOR THIS WEEK IS____

NOTE: Fill in any blanks as you go through the key statement blanks if you have not done so.

LESSON SIX
THE PREVENTION AND CARE WHICH WILL LEAD TO A HEALTHY NATION

Our main thrust in the final lessons is to give the prescription and care that may lead to national healing. We will attempt to do this by showing some foundational principles in raising a healthy new generation of workers. In order to accomplish this goal we must learn how to better care for our spiritual babies.

After examining the symptoms of a sick society, we determined that the Untied States has those symptoms and is a sick nation in the sight of God. We then turned to other periods of apostasies and studied their case histories in order to see if there was any hope for America.(+)

CASE HISTORY ONE

We learned from the case study of the patients that GOD PLACED IN ISOLATION that those who were well enough to continue their journey into the Promised Land were UNDER THE SAME MANDATE God had originally given on Mt. Sinai. God had not changed his purpose **because of their unbelief and rebellion.**

The message for our Sick Society is that we are still under the mandate found in Matthew

28:18-20. This means that a person cannot attend one service on Sunday morning, give an offering, and fulfill his duty of what God commanded him to do in keeping God's mandate. Going to church was never meant to be just for educating people, but it was for the purpose of TRAINING PEOPLE "TO DO".

CASE HISTORY TWO

The next case history revealed that periods of apostasy **occurred over and over again**.(+) We found that each period of apostasy became worse than the previous one until God performed A DRASTIC SURGICAL PROCEDURE which cured the problem. The nation of Israel regained its health and enjoyed its greatest success and glory under the guidance of King David.

CASE HISTORY THREE

Case history three revealed the darkest period of Israel's national life where **they had even lost the Bible.** They were totally, with the exception of a remnant, given over to false religions. Under the leadership of Josiah, who began **the reformation as a teenager,** they had national revival.

The greatest principle that shines from this corrupt society is that **God is still God and He can use anyone**, even a child, if that person loves and serves God with all of his heart and life. Although it was the darkest night in Israel's history, its message shines the brightest to ensuing generations.

ITS MESSAGE: Serve God with **all of your heart and obey the Bible** AND THEN GOD WILL HEAR AND HEAL.(+) Although the Jews were carried out of their land as slaves, Josiah's dedicated service too God led to the Gospel being spread throughout the world.

CASE HISTORY FOUR

Case history four comes from a broken heart, which God healed and comforted. In answer to his prayer, Apostle Paul was **totally rejected** in his dying hour. The overwhelming pain of this abandonment and then the healing and comfort Paul received from the Lord taught Paul **how to comfort Timothy and all other pastors** who would experience a falling away from their ministries. Not only did God heal Paul, but God also gave **him four simple and yet difficult steps** that would overcome the people's apostasy.(+)

The greatest lessons for our generation are the POSITIVE HOPE WE CAN HAVE, AND THE STEPS THAT ARE PROVIDED TO AID THE HEALING OF AMERICA.(+)

Prevention and Care

Let us examine some principles that are found in those four steps concerning the establishing of a solid foundation which will bring healing.

PREVENTION WHICH DEVELOPS GOOD HEALTH

The word prevention carries with it a negative tone, but when it is applied in a Biblical way, IT GIVES POSITIVE RESULTS.

PREVENTATIVE MEDICINE FOR POSITIVE HEALTH

In the past few years there has been a change in thinking concerning the best way to **keep patients healthy**. In past history, most of mankind went to a doctor **when they became ill**. Today's practice for the 65 million people over 55 years old who live in America is just the opposite; one goes to the **doctor to prevent becoming sick. There are annual check-ups of all descriptions,** which are designed to keep the patients well. **This method of prevention has also long been the acceptable practice concerning dental care**.

This has always been the biblical **practice in childcare.** In fact, the most famous and oft quoted verse in the Bible concerning childcare is Proverbs 22:6, which states:

> "Train up a child in the way he
> should go: and when he is old,
> he will not depart from it."

This principle is absolutely true in training healthy spiritual babies.

MOSES ESTABLISHED THE FOUNDATION OF CHILD DEVELOMENT

In Deuteronomy 6:1-9, God gave the principles, which, when followed, would raise a successful and happy generation of Godly and productive children.(+) God has never rescinded his command nor has he ever altered his perfect plan for raising a healthy generation.(+)

The plan has to begin by having **a healthy environment in the home when the child is born.** The focus and training is UPON THE CHILD. The role modeling of the parents, the environment of love, and the positive enforcement of truth are all-important elements in the child's training. **In the early years** he learns from observing the examples of those in his home.

THE POSITIVE MANDATE OF JESUS

In Matthew 28:19-20, the literal command of Jesus is, AS YOU GO MAKE (in keeping with the principle of raising a healthy generation)

BABIES INTO DISCIPLES.(+) These verses in
the light of raising a healthy generation of new
converts should be clear; we are to teach the
babies to observe or do all things. Literally,
teaching them to observe or do all things well
enough to train others.(+)

Isn't that what good, domestic parents
attempt to do with their children? They teach
their children to be good, happy, normal adults
who can raise some good, happy, normal
grandchildren.

THE STRESS IN THE PASTORAL COMMISSION

When Jesus left this earth, he had to
replace himself as the pastor of the first church.

In John 21:15-22, Jesus commissioned
Peter, the first senior pastor, by giving him
THREE DISTINCT CHARGES.(+) Each time
Jesus emphasizes the only motive, LOVE, which
will keep a man in the ministry. It is the love and
gratitude that a man has for what Jesus has done
for him that keeps him in the office, which
demands ones complete surrender and obedience.
It is **the love that God has for the lost, which
spills over into the heart** of his under-shepherd
that causes him **to love poor lost humanity.**
This love will keep him faithfully serving.

Those points, along with others that we do not have the time to mention, are the reason that Jesus asked Peter three times: "… **Simon, *son* of Jonas, lovest thou me?..**" The answer which Peter made, although it may not have been the quality or degree of love with which some believe Peter should have given, was always the positive—"… YEA, LORD; THOU KNOWEST THAT I LOVE THEE …"

Upon receiving this positive declaration, Jesus gave Peter three different charges. The first, **feed my lambs or babies** emphasizes the absolute need to start discipling and training sinners as soon as they are born again.(+) Following the principle of the positive mandate to "… Feed my lambs." is good preventative medicine that will lead to growing a healthy and happy new generation of workers.

FOCUS ON "THE ONE"

In our modern day churches, the pastor's focus is ON THE HERD. This is a necessity to a point because of his calling and the demands placed upon his office, but there is a danger of a pastor focusing only on the herd to the hurt of the individual sheep, particularly the new convert. **We are in the people business, not the church (herd) business.**

Prevention and Care

Please take a moment in your effort to build a healthy generation of disciples to consider **the power of one.**

One young man, Josiah, who became King as a child of eight years old, was used of God to bring courage and a great revival in Israel.(+)

The first chapter of the book of Daniel reveals four young men of **unusual faith and courage**. These four young men, namely; Daniel, Shadrach, Meshach, and Abednego BURST ON THE SCENE! In contrast to the darkness of those living around them **their courage and convictions were startling.**

What caused them to be such strong and courageous young men?

THE POWER OF ONE IS THE ANSWER!

"The power of one? What are you talking about? The power of one?"

The influence of one dedicated servant of God who loved **God with all of his heart and all of his soul** and vowed never to break the covenant of God **is the answer.**

These four young men were slaves who had been carried to Babylon from Jerusalem. Jerusalem was where **young Josiah inherited the most corrupt, idolatrous city** in Israel's history. He single handedly broke down all of the false idol altars, he destroyed the temples of the false gods, and restored Israel to the point of following the principles of God's Word once again.

Josiah's courage to follow God with all his heart **inspired four other young men to have the same courage and faith** to follow their Lord with all of their hearts and souls also. Their courage and faith was used by God to save tens of thousands of **others all over the world.**

The power of one little boy, if properly protected and discipled, could change our world.(+)

A BIG JOB FOR ONE PASTOR

If a pastor can visualize the power of one dedicated worker, he instantly realizes that there are not enough hours in the day for him to be able to do the job ALONE. HE MUST DEVELOP WORKERS whom he can enlist as big brothers or sisters to aid him in discipling his new babies.

TREAT THEM LIKE NEW CONVERTS

As a pastor, start a class to train dedicated members. Ask each one to go through *The Milk of the Word* book as if they were "new converts". You will serve over them as their role model, and they will take the part of a new convert. In order for them to have the experience of learning while going through the book, you will "show as well as teach" them. This will equip them to be able to be better role models when you appoint them to be over a new convert.(+)

Authors note: We have a book of lesson plans, which will aid this effort.

THE PARALLELS IN RAISING BABIES

Throughout the Bible, the Holy Spirit **uses physical principles to convey spiritual truth**.(+) This is especially true in his attempt to get his pastors to properly care for and develop new spiritual babies or converts. **If a pastor understands the proper procedure** of raising good, well adjusted, domestic children, and will **apply the same principles** to rearing spiritual children for Christ, then he will be very successful as a pastor.

Let us consider the following four principles in God's brilliant plan to develop a new convert into a strong man.

- **The principle of feeding**
- **The principle of protecting**
- **The principle of pacifying**
- **The principle of discipline**

THE PRINCIPLE OF FEEDING

In the scripture that contains the pastoral commission to Peter, the first pastor, we have a command to "… Feed my lambs." (John 21:15)

In this passage of scripture, Jesus asked Peter three times if Peter loved him. The common interpretation of why Jesus asked Peter **three times** if he loved him is that Peter had denied Jesus **three times.**

This may be true, but I sincerely doubt it.

Jesus was not speaking to Peter JUST AS A MAN, BUT HE WAS GIVING PETER THE PASTORAL COMMISSION.(+) This commission dealt with not only the responsibility of a pastor to feed the flock, **but how the feeding was to be done.**

Jesus divided the flock (local church) into three categories of members:(+)

- The lambs, babies or new converts
- The weak, or wounded sheep
- The strong, healthy, producing sheep that are strong in the Lord and the power of his might.

He not only divided the members into three classes of members, but HE GAVE PETER THREE SEPARATE CHARGES OF HIS RESPONSIBILITY OF FEEDING EACH GROUP.(+)

The question arises as to why he would divide the church into three separate groups and **give Peter a direct command** to feed each group? Each command was preceded by the question, **do you love me, Simon, son of Jonas?(+)** Having been a pastor or a full time preacher for almost 60 years, I suggest to you that THE ONLY MOTIVATION that will keep a pastor fully involved in the difficult job of pastoring one of God's flocks is **love for the Saviour**. In the first commission to the first pastor, **Jesus emphasized this truth by asking Peter three times, "... Simon, *son* of Jonas, lovest thou me? ..."** Upon Peter's affirmative answer, Jesus charged Peter with the responsibility of **feeding my lambs (or babies).**

LESSONS FROM FEEDING A
DOMESTIC BABY

Please consider the procedures, which are followed in feeding a domestic baby:

FIRST, the milk must be taken to the baby. As simple as this may be, it is absolutely true. The only way one can feed an infant his food is to take it to the baby.

SECOND, the baby must be hand fed until he grows enough to feed himself.

THIRD, the baby must be taught to feed himself before he can take his place with the rest of the family at the dinner table.

THESE PRINCIPLES ARE ABSOLUTELY TRUE IN FEEDING A NEW CONVERT. The one who gave birth to the lamb (mother sheep, a symbol for a Christian) has to take the milk to the lamb. If she doesn't nurse the lamb, it will die unless someone stands in and hand feeds the helpless lamb. **An older child of God can be trained** to take the milk of the Word to the new convert.(+) This same person rightly divides, or uses, the Word of God to hand feed the new convert. This process is followed until the new convert learns how to rightly divide the Word of God so he can feed himself.

AN ILLUSTRATION WHICH VISUALIZES FEEDING THE BABY

Use your imagination to visualize a baby being brought home from the hospital a day or two after its birth in the hospital.

Visualize a large family, which includes both grandparents, all of the immediate family; aunts and uncles, plus the cousins. Watch the entire family gather in a large living room to welcome the little fellow home.

Mother places him in a baby bed, which is surrounded by this loving and adoring family.

IN UNION THEY PROCLAIM, "WELCOME INTO OUR FAMILY!" We have been praying for you, and we are so glad to have you in our family.

Then the patriarch of the family speaks, "Now listen up, kid! You have a wonderful mother that places delicious food on the table every day in the morning, at noon, and again at night. **If you are serious about being part of our family,** when she puts the food on the table, **you come and get it."(+)**

If this were the traditional way of raising babies in today's society, the question for you to answer would be: **"How many of these little babies would survive?"** Your answer to this dumb question would be: "NONE!"

Another dumb question to illustrate the point is, after the baby dies, would that family go around and justify the loss of the baby by saying; "Have you ever seen so many sick, dying babies, **which are being born in these "last days"**, or would they follow the procedure of raising good, happy babies?

IT IS HAPPENING IN OUR CHURCHES

A person is saved and joins our church family. The members go around and shake the new convert's hand.

The unspoken message to the new convert is, "We have a good Pastor who really preaches God's Word. Every Sunday morning, Sunday night and Wednesday night he places rich, tasty, spiritual food on the table. If you are serious about being part of our church family, when it is placed on the table, you come and get it!"

Many new converts try it for a few weeks and then drop out of church. The traditional comment over the loss of new converts is, "Have you ever seen so many unfaithful, sickly people who profess to be saved **in the last days**?"

Do you believe we should justify the loss of new converts by blaming the last days, or do you believe we ought to go back to the biblical way of feeding and developing our spiritual babies?(+)

THE PRINCIPLE OF PROTECTION

When a baby is born into a family, the whole routine of the family is interrupted. Medical science says that the most important time of a person's life is **the first 48 hours after his birth.** How tragic it is that the vast number of pastors are not aware of the dangers the new convert faces within a short period after his birth into God's family.

After the rejoicing part of the new convert's decision is over, he is all but forgotten and left to fend for himself.

HE NEEDS PROTECTION FROM THE OLDER CHILDREN

When a baby is born into a family the older brothers and sisters love their little baby, but in their eagerness to manifest their love, they could injure him.

As strange as it seems, older Christians injure new converts more than anything else. Older members are the greatest cause for the new convert DROPPING OUT OF CHURCH.(+)

You may be startled by this statement and instantly inquire "WHY?".

A smaller child learns most of his lessons **by observing the actions of older people**, especially those of his older brothers and sisters. In our day where there is little or no commitment by the majority of the church family, **the new convert learns to do wrong** by watching the unfaithful and worldly examples of those who should be proper role models, but aren't.(+) He either tries to **imitate their compromising lives** and backslides, or, **he is disenchanted** by their non-Christian lifestyle and **quits**.

The careless lifestyles of these Christians are the greatest hindrance in developing healthy, new converts into strong, solid Christians.

REVERSE THE POWER OF
A BAD EXAMPLE

The power of a bad example destroys new converts. One can offset this disastrous effect on the new convert by protecting him. If the power of careless members who live a self-serving life knocks the new convert out of church, then one can hold and develop a new convert BY PLACING A GOOD ROLE MODEL OVER HIM IMMEDIATELY AFTER HE IS SAVED.

We will continue this thought in the next lesson.

POINTS TO PONDER

- ❖ All of the Case Histories reveal societies as bad or worse than ours.
- ❖ AFTER severe chastisements, a new generation immerged with moral courage.
- ❖ This new generation flourished until they failed to "observe to do" God's Word.
- ❖ The hope of healing lies in the development of strong, healthy Christians.
- ❖ The development of a strong healthy Christian must begin at birth.
- ❖ God gave these principles in his Word.
- ❖ If we follow these principles, God will heal our nation.

God's Cure for Our Nation

MONDAY
(Foundational Principles in Raising a Healthy Generation)

1. We studied their _____ histories in order to _____ if there was any _____ for America.
2. The next case history _____ that periods of _____ occurred _____ and _____ again.
3. Serve God with _____ of your _____ and _____ the Bible and then God will _____ and _____.
4. God healed Paul and _____ him four _____ and yet difficult _____ that would _____ their apostasy.
5. The _____ lessons for our generation are the hope we can have, and the _____ that are provided to aid the _____ of America.

TUESDAY
(Prevention Which Brings Good Health)
1. The word prevention when it is _____ in a _____ way, it gives _____ results.

Prevention and Care

2.   God gave the _____ which when_____ would raise a successful and _____ generation of _____and productive children.

3.   God   has   _____   rescinded   his _____ nor   has   he ever_____ his _____plan for raising a _____ generation.

4.   As you _____ make (in keeping with the _____ of raising a _____ generation) _____ into disciples.

5.   Literally, teaching them to _____ or do all things well _____ to _____others.

WEDNESDAY
(The Stress of The Pastoral Commission)

1.   Jesus _____ Peter, the first pastor by giving him _____ distinct _____.

2.   Feed   my   lambs   or   _____ emphasizes the _____ need to start _____   and   training _____ as soon as they are _____ again.

3.   One young man, Josiah, who became a King as a child of eight_____ old, was

God's Cure for Our Nation

used of God to bring _____ and a
great _____ in Israel.

4.   The power of _____ little boy, if properly
protected and _____, could change
our _____.

5.   This will _____ them to be able
to be better_____ models when you
_____ them over a new
_____.

THURSDAY
(The Parallels of Raising Babies)

1.   Throughout the _____ the Holy Spirit
uses _____ principles to
_____ spiritual truth.

2.   Jesus was _____ speaking to Peter
just as a _____, but he was
_____ Peter the _____
commission.

3.   Jesus _____ the flock
(local_____) into three _____
of members.

4.   He gave _____ three separate
_____ of his _____ of
feeding_____ group.

5.   Each _____ was _____
by the _____, do you
_____ me Simon, son of Jonas?

FRIDAY
(Lessons From Feeding a Domestic Baby)

1.   An _____ child of God can be _____ to take the_____of the Word to the new _____.

2.   If you are _____ about being part of our _____, when she _____ the food on the table, you _____ and get it.

3.   Should we blame the _____days or go back to the _____ way of _____ and developing our spiritual babies?

4.   Older _____ are the _____ cause for the new convert _____ out of church.

5.   The convert _____ to do_____ by _____the unfaithful and _____ examples of those who should be _____ role models, but aren't.

Daily Declaration
If we will rock our new converts cradle and develop them, God will heal our nation.

MY COMMIMMENT

Regardless of how dark our day may become because of terrorist attracts, I will work to be part of our nation's healing.

Name: _____

Memory Verse

John 15:16

"Ye have not chosen me, but I have chosen you, and ordained you, that ye should go and bring forth fruit, and *that* your fruit should remain: that whatsoever ye shall ask of the Father in my name, he may give it you."

	M	T	W	TH	F	S	S
AM							
PM							

- **GIVE YOURSELF AN "A"** if you filled in and reviewed the blanks on a daily basis. This will raise your potential of remembering on an average to 62%
- **GIVE YOURSELF A "B"** if you completed all your blanks before class time.
- **GIVE YOURSELF A "J" FOR JUDGMENT** in order to remind yourself that one has to give account of each day's activity when he takes his finals at the judgment seat of Christ

Prevention and Care

MY GRADE FOR THIS WEEK IS____

NOTE: Fill in any blanks as you go through the key statement blanks if you have not done so.

LESSON SEVEN
THE DEVELOPMENT OF NEW CONVERTS

In this chapter we will deal with some positive principles for developing our baby brothers and sisters into good happy members of God's family. We closed our last lesson by introducing the biblical concept of placing a proper role model over the new convert as soon as he is saved.

The proper role model has several duties to the new convert, but his main purpose is to protect and offset the effect of other professed Christians who live a self-serving life and who are bad examples to the new convert.(+)

A DEFINITION OF A GOOD ROLE
MODEL IS ONE WHO IS:

- Dedicated to the Lord
- Loyal to the pastor
- Faithful to all services
- Sound in the Scriptures
- Sweet in Spirit
- Diligent in his service to the new convert

This role model is appointed over the new convert and his job is to befriend and **work with the new convert as the pastor may direct**.

This spiritual role model **sits with the new convert** whenever it is possible. The role model looks for him in all services and introduces him to new people.(+) He explains to the convert what is going on in order to make him feel comfortable and accepted in his new family.

THE TREATMENT OF NEW CONVERTS AND THE DEVELOPMENT OF DISCIPLE-MAKERS

The pastor is charged with the responsibility of caring for the new converts and with the responsibility of developing disciple-makers. These two responsibilities, although very similar, are quite different.

Caring for the new convert is the heart of these lessons.(+) Each new convert should be given special care and attention. He should be given instructions as soon as he is born. If the person will permit it, a role model should be placed over him.

SOME PEOPLE WILL NOT ACCEPT BEING DISCIPLED

One does not know another person's heart and the Bible warns against judging people, but there is a certain type of believer, (as well as can be discerned), that is saved but refuses to be discipled.(+)

One of the main reasons for this failure to be discipled is the destruction that comes to people's initiative and character through the government welfare programs. Many do not have enough character to break out of the lifestyle they have been in all of their lives. There is also the possibility that they were not really saved when they made their profession.

There was a similar situation in the ministry of Apostle Paul. Although it was different in some ways, the principle was the same. When people refused the word of God and the help which was offered, Paul said, **"... seeing ye put it from you [the offered help], and judge yourselves unworthy of everlasting life, lo, we turn to the Gentiles [others]."** Acts 13:46 The principle demonstrated here is one cannot help people unless they want it. Do not continue to try and help a person if he is not responsive—turn to others who will accept help.

DISCIPLE-MAKERS MUST BE FAITHFUL MEN

It is very clear in the Bible that disciple-makers should be "faithful men" (II Tim 2:2) and "faithful women".

Luke 14:26-33 states three times that unless people meet certain conditions, although they may be saved, they could not be his disciples.

A person must be faithful and love the Lord enough to put him first in his life in order to be discipled into a disciple-maker. God commands each of his children to become a disciple-maker. However, a person should not waste his time trying to disciple a person who is not faithfully committed to the Lord. One cannot teach or disciple a person unless you have their heart and cooperation.(+)

But keep in mind, we have a better chance of making people into disciple-makers if we start our training the moment they accept Christ.

PASTORS ARE PRESSURED
INTO BAD HABITS

The pastor's life is not his own.(+) There are all kinds of demands made on his time. Sunday is the busiest time of the week. He works all week in preparation for the Sunday services.

When the pastor finishes one service, he has to instantly focus on the next one. Perhaps there is a counseling session with someone with a problem. There is his family who needs the attention and love of their father and husband. It could be some other item which **demands his immediate attention**.

So when the invitation is over and people are saved, he rejoices! **God has voted on and blessed all the efforts he made** during the week. When the dismissal prayer has ended with a echo of amens his mind GOES TO THE NEXT scheduled event(+) – dinner with family or friends, counseling or there is the next service to be prepared which demands his complete attention. Although his thoughts are thankful and he has full intention of meeting with his new converts **he has to rush on to perform his never-ending duties.**

A WAY TO PROTECT THE
NEW CONVERT

When the person saved makes his profession of salvation, give him a booklet with important instructions. In the booklet there is **a new birth certificate**. Fill in the new birth certificate and spend about five minutes explaining the important truths he must understand **for his own GOOD AND PROTECTION**.

After these brief instructions, make an appointment within the next seven days (the sooner the better) to go over the book with him.(+) The one presenting the book has been given the times that **the pastor or staff can meet**

with the new converts so they can make the appointment on their behalf.

SALVATION IS AN EMOTIONAL EXPERIENCE. Salvation is an experience because He has been born again. It is emotional because he has the JOY of forgiven sins. **Without the instruction of the booklet,** which informs him of the attack of the devil, his own human (fleshly) feelings, and the sometimes negative reaction of family members and friends, **the new convert is set up for a fall.(+)**

All the devil has to do to confuse or stop him in his Christian growth is to **GIVE HIM ANOTHER EMOTIONAL EXPERIENCE!** The devil does this by getting him to commit a sin or provoke him to lose his temper. This will throw him into confusion and cause him to draw back, or at least hesitate in following Christ.

He had an emotional experience when he received Christ. He felt so good! The guilt and condemnation was gone; he felt so happy and now...HE BLEW IT! He reasons within himself, "Am I lost again?" (Many churches teach that he is.) If I haven't lost my salvation by sinning, AT THE LEAST I AM A VERY WEAK CHRISTIAN. I need to get better than I am before I make any other big decisions (baptism). His confidence (faith) is shaken. He begins to wonder… "Maybe this Christian business is not for me…"

We must help this new convert who has just been saved and is **still living out in the sick society**. He is still on shaky ground and unsure of himself. Everything is so new (to him). The devil brings to his memory the warnings he has been given about "those Baptists". This unsettled condition all began when he was saved. The church left him with only an **EMOTIONAL EXPERIENCE,** and did not prepare him for the attacks of the devil, the flesh, and the reaction of some of his friends.

THE HELP AND PROTECTIONS
HE NEEDS

Having dealt with people both at the altar and in the home for almost 60 years, I have learned about the pitfalls a new convert faces upon his decision to receive Christ.

After the joy he experienced in receiving Christ has been expressed and he begins to resume his regular activities, the devil begins to shoot thoughts of doubts into his mind.

"What did you let those **people talk you into**?"

"**You sure have done it now…You can never have any more fun…You will probably** become a preacher or a monk…All they want is your money…"

It has been years since I led anyone to the Lord that I have not warned the new believer of the attacks of the devil.

I would generally say, "When I go **out the front** door, the old devil is going to **come in the back door**." Then I would take a few minutes and fill in the details of how the devil would attack and I would finish by asking, "What are you going to tell the old devil?" The answer I was after was, "**that soul winner didn't talk me into anything, ole devil! Because I received Jesus as my Saviour and I am going to heaven when I die!**"

After going through this procedure for a number of years, I came to realize that the new convert needed printed material to help him ward off the attacks of the devil and help him start his new life for Christ. He needed help **from the point of his decision to become a Christian until he was successfully serving Christ in a local church under a pastor**. So I wrote the booklet entitled, "**From Salvation to Service**".

There are now over 150,000 of these booklets somewhere in the world. After filling out the birth certificate in the front of the book, and helping him to see that his name was written in the Lamb's Book of Life in heaven, he needed to know seven things that would greatly strengthen the **Emotional Experience** he had when he received Christ.(+)

THE PRINCIPLE OF
PACIFYING THE BABY

A natural baby needs more than proper food and protection in order to grow into a healthy, well-adjusted person. He needs someone in a healthy environment to make him feel secure and loved.(+) We use the term PACIFY because in the Spanish language THE PASTORAL COMMISSION "FEED MY LAMBS" reads with the stress of more than just feeding the lambs. We are to make them feel secure and happy. A baby needs more than food in order to grow into a healthy baby that is emotionally sound. A further study of this pastoral commission gives the emphasis of **tending to my lambs**. In order for us to comprehend how to feed or care for the lambs, God chose to use terms which indicated the similarities between developing good, healthy, well adjusted, domestic babies and developing good, healthy, spiritual babies.(+)

To pacify my babies means we are to help the new convert to have a peaceful, secure environment in which to grow. A pastor does this by placing an older brother or sister over the new convert to work with and serve as his role model.

The role model gives a weekly report so the pastor can be informed of the new convert's progress and need. The pastor then knows how to direct the role model in his work. The role model carries a message to the new convert each week that reveals the pastor's love and concern.

Members also have a responsibility in developing the converts, or babies, in their church family.(+) They will also have to answer at the judgment seat as to the way they responded to the protection and needs of other members, especially the babes in Christ.

ADOPT A BABY

Many homes are empty because there are no children. Nothing brightens up a home more than a happy, contented baby does. As a responsible member of the church, one should CONSIDER ADOPTING A SPIRITUAL BABY. Introduce yourself and get acquainted with the new convert when the person first accepts Christ. Invite him to have dinner with you. Discuss spiritual things and make him feel proud of his decision. Become knowledgeable of "**The Salvation to Service Booklet**", and help him to fully comprehend the principles in the booklet.

Paul talks about different young ministers and calls them "**sons**". John refers to his converts as his **children**. Why don't you adopt a son or daughter that you can put your life into? Why don't you start praying about it and ask God to direct you to someone? I am not suggesting that you start praying about it and then sit down and wait for something to happen. **Get involved in helping new converts until your special baby comes along**.(+)

VOLUNTEER TO BECOME
A NURSERY WORKER

Your response may be, "**Me? A nursery worker**?" Before you reject the idea as something below your level of service, consider the one who started and was in charge of the nursery of the First Baptist Church of the Thessalonians. It was the senior pastor and founder of the church, **the apostle Paul.** Speaking of his duties and service in the spiritual nursery Paul said:

"But we were gentle among you, EVEN AS A NURSE CHERISHETH her children: So being affectionately desirous of you, we were willing to have imparted unto you, not the gospel of God only, but also our own souls, because ye were dear unto us." I Thessalonians 2:7-8

Paul's work in the nursery with the new converts established the foundation of the greatest church of all the churches found in the New Testament.

Working with the newborn babes in Christ might become **the greatest decision and investment** you ever made.(+) It would not only give you rich and lasting gratification in your present life, but it would lead to a relationship of joy and pride that would make you the great winner **both now and forever!**

THE PRINCIPLE OF DISCIPLINE

There is little or no discipline of children in many American homes today. With both father and mother working a full time job outside the home, the children are left without a structured life. Much of the children's training is left up to the church or school.(+) The result is that many of them are nothing less than spoiled children who clamor for mom and dad's time and attention. Many of them have grown up and have never been taught how to work or live under discipline.

This is another aspect found in our sick society. It is from this environment of no discipline that we must establish **the principle of discipline** in the lives of new converts.(+)

HOW CAN WE ESTABLISH DISCIPLINE?

The question arises, "How can we establish discipline in the lives of new converts who have been raised in an undisciplined society?" To use an expression which has already been quoted once in this writing "… With men this is impossible; BUT WITH GOD ALL THINGS ARE POSSIBLE." Matthew 19:26b(+)

DISCIPLINE MUST START AT THE POINT OF THEIR NEW BIRTH

The problem of undisciplined children did not originate with the children. It is the parents of the children who are the cause for the break down of discipline in the home.

If parents of a child begin to establish discipline in the life of their baby in a loving way when the child is born, they will raise a person who will always be their pride and joy. But, if they wait until the child is 10-12 years old before attempting to train him, they will raise a heartbreak.

THE SAME IS TRUE IN RAISING A SPIRITUAL BABY. We must begin instilling discipline in the lives of our spiritual babies the moment they receive Christ.(+)

The problem with the parents in our modern day society is that they have rejected **God's holy manual**, which gives the instructions on raising good children. The same can be said about most of the pastors and churches of America. We are involved with the **traditional practices of our present day** instead of following the clear teaching found in OUR OPERATIONAL MANUAL concerning raising good, healthy, DISCIPLINED NEW CONVERTS.(+)

The literal instructions found in the mandate of Jesus in the Gospel of Matthew are **as you go, make men into disciples**. (28:19) The following verse (20) instructs the taking of disciples **to the level where they can observe, do or practice** the principles well enough to train others. This principle MUST BE COMMUNICATED TO THE BABY AS SOON AS HE IS BORN.

PLEASE CONSIDER A MORE DELIBERATE APPROACH

The better practice, as indicated in the mandate of making disciples, is to work with the lost person, when possible, to teach him the responsibility of a Christian BEFORE HE IS SAVED.(+) One can do this in an informal Bible study with the person on a weekly basis. It could be a "one on one" session or in a group setting. One pastor, who has built a great discipling church, meets with a person each week. They

begin in the first chapter of the Gospel of John
and together read one chapter each session until
the person understands what a Christian is, and
how he is to live after receiving Christ. The
pastor testified, "The furthest I have gone through
the gospel of John was chapter seventeen before
the person was saved." After the person is saved,
he turns him over to a big brother who continues
the discipling process.(+) There have been many
who have gone out from his church to serve in
other places while his large work force of men
continues to grow.

You may wonder, "Why does he take the
more deliberate approach to soul-winning?"

- ❖ **He is following** a method to win the
  whole family, not just a single member
  of the family.(+)
- ❖ **He is following** a method, which grows
  strong, healthy members, who have the
  possibility of multiplying.
- ❖ **He is following** a method that is more
  in harmony with the pattern found in the
  New Testament.
- ❖ **He is following** a method, **observe to
  do,** which has the potential of making
  America healthy once again.

The process of disciplining or making disciples should be planted in the heart of the new convert as soon as possible. He should be instructed that he is to learn the principles he is being taught well enough to teach others. The older Christian should work with the new convert in showing him how to serve God as well as in teaching him how to serve God.

FILL THE GREATEST NEED OF OUR DAY

The greatest need of our day, as we minister to the people of our sick society, is to realize that God has given instructions in his OPERATIONAL MANUAL which will bring revival to our churches if we will follow them.

A wise man named Solomon once concluded his findings on "what is the purpose for man on this earth" with some words we will borrow and paraphrase.

He said, "... **Fear God, and keep his commandments ...**" He then explained why one should fear God and keep his commandments. It was because God would bring **all the works into judgment, whether the works were good or bad.** (Ecclesiastes 12:13-14). Those words are fitting, and should be applied to the principle of raising healthy new converts who will grow to help us restore a healthy, spiritual climate once again in our churches. We can do this by training a new generation

- We must seek God's guidance in "not inducing labor" prematurely.
- We must protect our new converts or babies in order to develop them.
- We must focus on the power of One, and thus work with individuals.- Josiah's devotion to God, lead to the courage and faith of Daniel and the three Hebrew children which caused the Gospel to be preached to the whole world. Backslidden Lot's son, Moab, grew into a nation which God destroyed two hundred years later because of their idolatry.
- We must learn to take the milk of God's Word to our babies and hand feed them until they learn to feed and care for themselves.
- We must pacify or help them to feel loved and secure as we involve them in our church family.
- We must follow the principles, which will help them learn to work under discipline.
- We must teach them that their purpose is to learn the principles of God **well enough to train others.**(+)

The Development of New Converts

God has promised to bless his Word when his children meet his conditions for his honor and glory. Our mandate is clear "**as ye go, make men into disciples.**" If we obey this command, WE MUST START BY PROTECTING AND DEVELOPING HIS BABIES.(+) We must realize that time is short and our cause is urgent. We will meet each day's activity again at the judgment. May God help us to protect and develop a new generation of healthy Christian workers.

POINTS TO PONDER

❖ The most important time in the life of a baby is his first 48 hours.

❖ The loss of new converts is the most discouraging loss which a church suffers.

❖ A spiritual baby needs protection and love as well as spiritual food to develop properly.

❖ A role model must be placed over him as soon as he is saved.

The Development of New Converts

MONDAY
(The Development of new converts)

1. The proper _____ model has _____ duties to the new _____, but his _____ purpose is to _____.

2. The role model _____ for him in the _____ and _____ him to new people.

3. Caring for the _____ convert is the _____ of these lessons.

4. There is a _____ type of believer who _____ to be discipled.

5. One can _____ teach or disciple a person _____ you have their _____ and _____.

TUESDAY
(Pastors are pressured into bad habits)

1. The Pastors _____ is not his _____.

2. When the _____ prayer has _____ his mind goes to the _____ scheduled _____.

3. Make an _____ within the next _____ days (the sooner the

_____) to go over the book
_____ him.

4.   Without the _____ of the booklet
the new convert is _____ up for a
_____.

5.   The new convert needs to _____
seven things which will greatly _____
the emotional _____ he had when he
_____ Christ.

WEDNESDAY
(The Principle of Pacifying the Baby)

1.   He needs someone in a _____
environment to make him feel _____
and _____.

2.   God chose terms which _____ the
_____ between developing domestic
babies and _____. _____
good spiritual _____.

3.   Members also _____ a
_____ in developing _____
or babies.

4.   Get involved in _____ new
converts until your _____ baby comes
along.

5.   Working with newborn _____ might
become the greatest _____ and
_____ you ever made.

THURSDAY
(The Principle of Discipline)

1. Much of the _____ training is left up to the _____ or _____.

2. It is from this _____ of no discipline that we _____ establish the principle of _____.

3. With men this is _____ but with God _____ things are _____.

4. We must begin _____ discipline in the lives of our spiritual _____ the _____ they receive Christ.

5. We are involved with the _____ practice of our present day instead of _____ the teaching in our operational _____.

FRIDAY
(Please Consider more Deliberate Approach)

1. Work with the _____ person, when possible, to teach him the _____ of a Christian _____ he is saved.

2. After he is _____, he turns him over to a _____ brother who continues the process.

God's Cure for Our Nation

3. He is _____ a _____ to win the _____ family, not just a _____ member of the family.
4. We must teach them that their _____ is to _____ the principles of God _____ enough to _____ others.
5. If we _____ this _____ we must start by _____ and _____ his babies.

Daily Declaration

THE SURVIVAL OF OUR NATION DEPENDS UPON GOD'S PEOPLE PROTECTING AND TRAINING OUR SPIRITUAL BABES INTO STRONG WORKERS.

MY COMMIMMENT

I will break with the traditional way of ignoring our spiritual babies and become an active protector and disciplers of new converts.

Name: _____

The Development of New Converts

Memory Verse

Proverbs 22:6
"Train up a child in the way he should go: and when he is old, he will not depart from it."

	M	T	W	TH	F	S	S
AM							
PM							

- **GIVE YOURSELF AN "A"** if you filled in and reviewed the blanks on a daily basis. This will raise your potential of remembering on an average to 62%
- **GIVE YOURSELF A "B"** if you completed all your blanks before class time.
- **GIVE YOURSELF A "J" FOR JUDGMENT** in order to remind yourself that one has to give account of each day's activity when he takes his finals at the judgment seat of Christ

MY GRADE FOR THIS WEEK IS____

NOTE: Fill in any blanks as you go through the key statement blanks if you have not done so.

LESSON EIGHT
THERAPY WHICH PRODUCES HEALING

Just as God has always had a positive command "to observe to do" which brought his blessings he also has steps in therapy which would bring healing.

"Then shall thy light break forth as the morning, and THINE HEALTH SHALL SPRING FORTH SPEEDILY: and thy righteousness shall go before thee; the glory of the Lord shall be thy rereward." Isaiah 58:8(+)

In the following verse he continues by promising, "**Then shalt thou call,** and the Lord shall answer; **thou shalt cry**, and he (God) shall say, **Here I** *am ...*"

GOD WILL HEAL AND MAKE FRUITFUL

The abundant promise of spiritual fruit denotes winning and discipling the new convert which reaches the level of spiritual multiplication.(+) Please read and study God's descriptive promise in verse twelve.

"And *they that shall be* of thee **SHALL BUILD THE OLD WASTE PLACES**: thou shalt raise up the foundations of **many generations**; and thou shalt be called, The repairer of the breach, The restorer of paths to dwell in."

Therapy Which Produces Healing

Notice, "... *they that shall be of thee* ..." or your spiritual children shall build the old waste places (reopen churches which were closed). Thou (your spiritual children) shalt raise up the foundations (moral, Godly, and Biblical) of many generations. This undoubtedly is referring to making babies into disciples **who will be able to teach others** who will teach others...(+)

Thou shalt be called (as Moses, Paul, and others were) the repairers of the breach, the restorer of paths (biblical paths) to dwell (live) in.

There are two or three other major promises which God makes to Israel in this same chapter. The last of which deals with one's reward and **position in the millennial reign.**

UNLIMITED BLESSINGS IN THIS LIFE AND ON THROUGH THE MILLENNIUM

What makes these tremendous promises so much more glorious is they are promises which are conditional. IT IS A PROMISE OF BLESSING OR DESTRUCTION.(+)

❖ It is either **one** or the **other**
❖ It is **destruction** or **healing**
❖ **God promises are conditional and immutable**

Therapeutic treatment, which brings about healing, is often very difficult. It is taxing to one's strength and challenges one's determination to get well.

The principles that the people of a nation have to follow in order to regain moral strength and godliness can only be performed by God's grace and help. **Please ponder his emphatic promise to Israel.**

There are certain conditions to be met in order for God to heal.(+) These conditions **are immutable or unchangeable** which means that when ever a nation meets these conditions, whether the nation is Israel or America, God must take action. God not only longs to do so (heal) but he has taken an oath upon his own honor that he would.

Please read Isaiah 58:14 and see God's immutable promise of millennial blessings.

"Then [when the conditions are met] shalt thou delight thyself in the Lord; and I will cause thee to ride upon the high places of the earth, and feed thee with the heritage [millennial] of Jacob thy father: for the mouth of the Lord has spoken *it.*" The promise is so unbelievable that God first states it and then reaffirms it by concluding: "... **the mouth of the Lord hath spoken *it.*"**

Please understand our options as a nation! It is both **judgments** and **destruction** or IT IS HEALING AND BE DELIGHTED BY GOD.

The difficult therapy that God has prescribed are found in this chapter also. They are spirit filled exercises which are very different for God's people to perform. But if America is to escape the wrath and judgment of God because of our wickedness especially the way we have ignored his spiritual babies we must begin to perform these spiritual exercises at once. We can win and then develop our spiritual babies **if we will humble ourselves and perform** the following spiritual exercises.

- ❖ **God's preachers must preach**
- ❖ **God's people must practice biblical fasting and prayer.**
- ❖ **God's people must honor the Lord's Day.**

GOD'S PREACHERS MUST PREACH

Many of God's true preachers have gotten into bad habits when it comes to preaching! We call it preaching because they call it preaching, but what many call preaching should be called teaching while others should be called performances. Many take their favorite notebook which they compiled while they were in college and use it to teach a series of lessons. Most of these messages may be factual and true to the Bible but has no convicting power or life. It aims at nothing but the presenting of the Word which leaves most of the people empty and unchallenged or fat and (spiritually) lazy.

This type of preaching must change if America is TO BE CHANGED(+).

I can hear some preacher say, "You have your style and I have my style".

Other preachers will say, "My preaching is me. It expresses my personality. That is who I am and if people don't like it they can go somewhere else."

My answer to those preachers who feel that way is, "If you can find that pattern for your type of preaching in the Bible then keep doing it.(+) If you cannot it would be wise to change."

LET US NOTE THE PRESCRIBED PREACHING WHICH WILL PRODUCE HEALING IN OUR NATION.

PREACH AND NOT TEACH

Perhaps the most noted teacher of our day (by radio) and in the past generation was Dr. J. Vernon McGee. But Dr. McGee knew the difference **between preaching and teaching**. He was one of the most powerful, spirit filled preachers I ever knew. (Yes, I knew J. Vernon McGee).

PREACHING WITH FORCE AND POWER

The type of preaching that will bring healing is commanded in Isaiah 58:1 which proclaims,

"Cry aloud, spare not, lift up thy voice like a trumpet, and shew my people their transgression[+], and the house of Jacob their sins."

John the Baptist followed this order of preaching to bring healing in his dark day.

Matthew 3:1 declares that John came "… preaching [the Greek word for preaching means bellowing like an ox] in the wilderness of Judea,"

John preached repentance and his preaching against sin, caused him to lose his life. Jesus' comment about John and his preaching was (paraphrase) **there was not one born of a woman any greater**.

OUR PERFECT ROLE MODEL
FOR PREACHERS

Jesus was the perfect preacher. After preaching for two or three years Jesus asked the apostles what people were saying about his ministry. (Matthew 16:13). Their answer indicated the style of preaching Jesus did.

SOME SAY YOU ARE JOHN THE BAPTIST

Why do you believe they would think that Jesus was John the Baptist? The answer is obvious, Jesus preached like John the Baptist. He cried aloud, and made his voice like a trumpet (clear and plain with a distinct message) and preached against sin.

SOME SAY YOU ARE A ELIJAH

What made Elijah the Old Testament prophet famous? Elijah was noted because of his powerful spirit filled messages. Elijah was so known for the empowering of the Holy Spirit upon his life that Elisha wanted a double portion of "thy spirit". Jesus, our model preacher was a spirit filled preacher.

SOME SAY YOU ARE JEREMIAH.

Jeremiah was known as a weeping and compassionate preacher.(+) The way Jesus preached caused some to think he was the weeping prophet Jeremiah.

SOME SAY YOU ARE ONE
OF THE PROPHETS

Perhaps, they didn't know the Bible well enough to compare Jesus to a particular preacher but they knew a preacher when they heard one. By the way, what are people saying about your style of preaching? Better yet, what will Jesus say to you at the judgment seat when you answer to him about "your style" of ministry.

PREACH WITH HOLY SPIRIT POWER

Please read the purpose of preaching in verse six. It was to;

- ❖ "To loose the bonds of wickedness" – Save harden sinners, Please note that these types of sinners will be saved under sprit-filled preaching. This means that if the reader has someone who is described in the list of hardened sinners there is hope for that person.
- ❖ "To undo the heavy burdens" – The burden of alcohol, drugs, sex, and religion
- ❖ "To let the oppressed go free" – Addicts were made free men
- ❖ "To break every yoke" – Bring every sinner to his knees, cleanse him and set him free as a testimony to God's grace and power.

Teaching or nominal preaching will not cure these types of addictions; depression and religious yokes as described in verse six. It will take the power of God through spirit filled preaching.(+) All of the apostles had completed their Bible college training and had served their **training as interns** but Jesus commanded them **to tarry in Jerusalem until they were endued with Holy Spirit power.** Why? Because in order to be effective as a preacher it takes more than education and the knowledge of how to preach. It takes the Holy Spirit working through a preacher as he delivers God's message.

PREACH WITH COMPASSION

With the sinner suspended between heaven and eternal hell how could anyone be content with "just giving them a good homiletical message?"

People are blinded by sin and religion, bound by habits and addiction and condemned to suffer forever in hell unless they are persuaded to repent of their sins and be born again.

People in this condition were commanded by God to be preached to WITH COMPASSION.(+) His words were, "**And if thou draw out thy soul to the hungry, and satisfy the afflicted soul ...**" This literally means, "Pour out your heart" or, **preach with your heart**, PREACH WITH COMPASSION, and imitate Jesus and the apostle Paul who went night and day WITH TEARS. (Acts 20:31) As one who searches the Bible he will find men who "goeth forth with tears" preaching God's Word with compassion. For heaven's sake brother, people are headed for eternal ruin in hell; Jesus gave his life in order to save them. It will take a messenger with compassion and power to change them So Preach, **Preach, PREACH!**(+)

GOD'S PEOPLE MUST PRACTICE BIBLICAL PRAYER AND FASTING

The discussion between God and that generation of Jews shows the confusion concerning fasting (going without food)(+). This confusion about fasting prevails even to our day.

In verse three the Jews complain to God by saying, "Wherefore [why] have we fasted, *say they* [the Jews] and thou [God] seest not? *wherefore* [why] have we afflicted our soul, and thou takest no knowledge?.."(+)

God answers their complaint and questions in verses three, four and five by saying

- ❖ The day you fast is like a normal day in which you find pleasure. You are only doing it so you can say, "I fasted."
- ❖ In the day of your fast it is business as usual "you exact all labor" or work like it was any other day.
- ❖ You bow your heads as a bulrush bush in order to make a show of fasting

❖ You spread sack cloth and ashes under you to be noticed by others

❖ You fast for strife and debate-that is, you fast in order to win an argument and get your way.

THE PROPER REASONS FOR FASTING

The reasons for fasting and the rewards for doing so are plainly presented in this chapter.

FAST IN ORDER TO GET YOUR PRAYERS ANSWERED

Notice the main reason for fasting is to MAKE YOUR PRAYERS KNOWN ON HIGH(+) (verse four). Isaiah gives further instruction on prayer and fasting and concludes by giving God's promise.

"Then shalt thou call, [pray], and the Lord shall answer; thou shalt cry [because of fear or adversity], and he shall say, **Here I *am* ...**" (verse nine)

Throughout the Bible in days of great need or crisis one will see people gather together, not only to pray but to **fast and pray.**(+)

FAST IN ORDER TO HAVE POWER FOR SOUL WINNING AND SERVICE(+)

Again the description of the four types of sinners described in verse six are difficult cases.

They are sinners who are bound by wickedness. They are people with heavy burdens. They are sinners oppressed by witchcraft and false religions. They are sinners yoked up as leaders of false religions or very involved with idolatry. They needed the power of God to break their yoke and sin. The inspired writer states the purpose of fasting. The purpose of fasting is illustrated in the ministry of Jesus. He had a special service with John, James and Peter upon the mount of transfiguration. While they were up there a man brought his son to the disciples to be healed. They failed to heal the son! When Jesus came down from the Mountain he healed the man's son.

After the service was over his disciples who had failed in their attempts to heal the son questioned Jesus about their failure.

"... Why could not we cast him out?" (Matthew 17:19)

Jesus' answer was, "Because of your unbelief ..." and continuing, he explained by saying, "Howbeit this kind goeth not out but **by prayer and fasting**."(+) Matthew 17:21 In times of apostasy people become more addicted to sin. Alcohol and the use of all types of narcotics cause people to degenerate into harden criminals. Religion grips people like a steel vice! In order to break through to them it takes the power of God.

The type of power which comes only through periods of prayer and fasting. The therapy of prayer and fasting is one of the most difficult spiritual exercises for people to do but if there is ever to be healing of our nation...IT MUST BE DONE!(+)

GOD'S PEOPLE MUST LEARN TO HAVE COMPASSION AS THEY MINISTER TO THE POOR

In today's society people turn a blind eye to others who are in need or distress.

Shortly after Penny and I moved to Espanola I was using canal water to irrigate my lawn. In order to turn the water from the canal into our small ditch I had to cross the unimproved street in front of our property. After opening the Watergate which came to our property I started down the steep bank, stepped on a loose rock and fell. In my attempt to regain my balance and not fall I ended up falling very hard right out in the middle of the road; it really stunned me, and caused me to go to numerous doctors for several months. As I lay out in the middle of the city street two cars slowly passed by without stopping to offer any help. Later as I considered why no one offered an old man any assistance I came to the conclusion, they must have thought I was drunk!

Fasting while seeking God's face in prayer was designed by God to soften our hearts toward the need of other poor struggling people.(+)

Please note one of the sinful practices which one must stop in order to be used and blessed of God. The words "yoke" and the "putting forth of the finger" reveal a false standard of righteousness which some impose on others (v.9) and a critical attitude which they have for those who do not measure up to their standards. Some people must heed the admonishment of Jesus about getting the "beam" out of their own eye before imposing a yoke upon a brother by pointing out his short-comings. This spirit greatly hinders ones prayers.

Isaiah continues talking about prayer and fasting in verse seven. The verse says:

"*Is it* not to deal thy bread to the hungry, and that thou bring the poor that are cast out to thy house? when thou seest the naked, that thou cover him; and that thou hide not thyself from thine own flesh?"

❖ Have compassion as you deal your bread to the poor – have mercy and help the poor struggling masses(+)

❖ Bring people into your house that have been cast out or evicted. Help them in their need, minister the word to them while they are hurting.

❖ Cover the nakedness of the less fortunate by giving them clothes(+)

❖ Help those of your own family who are in need. Show the true spirit of Christ to the less fortunate of your extended family.

These examples teach us to look for people who are hurting and help them. This is the spirit of real Christianity and gives great opportunity to display the spirit and love of Christ. This tender loving help will lead to winning souls. Instead of living unto ourselves in our warm houses and enjoying materialistic blessings which come from God we should have compassion upon the hurting and use those facilities and substances to serve and help the poor.(+)

The next verse tells of God's blessings upon his OBEDIENT SERVANTS WHO WOULD DO SO; of having compassion upon the poor in using the things which God gave to relieve their distress and need, God promises, "Then shall thy light break forth as the morning, and thine **health shall spring forth speedily** …"(+)

POINTS TO PONDER

❖ America will be **severely punished,** if not destroyed unless **God intervenes.**

❖ God has stated the **conditions for America to meet to** prevent this judgment.

❖ His spiritual therapy demands sprit-filled preaching **by his preachers.**

❖ His spiritual therapy demands **fasting and praying by his people.**

❖ His spiritual therapy demands that his people minister **with compassion and tears**.

❖ His spiritual therapy will not be possible **unless people honor** the Lord's day.

❖ His spiritual therapy demands **protecting and developing** His babies into a strong work force which **will bring healing to America.**

MONDAY
(Therapy Which Produces Healing)

1. "Then shall thy _____ break forth as the morning, and THINE _____ SHALL SPRING FORTH _____:

2. The abundant promise of spiritual fruit denotes _____ and _____ the new convert which reaches the level of spiritual multiplication.

3. This undoubtedly is referring to _____ babies into _____ **who will be able to teach others** who will _____ others…

4. IT IS A _____ OF BLESSING OR _____

5. There are certain _____ to be _____ in order for God to _____.

TUESDAY
(God's Preachers must preach)

1. **This type of** _____ **must change if** _____ **is TO BE** _____.

2. "If you can _____ that pattern for
   _____ _____ type of preaching in the
   _____ then keep
   _____ it.

3. "**Cry** _____, _____
   not, lift up thy _____ like a
   trumpet, and _____ my
   people their transgression, and the house of
   Jacob their _____.

4. Jeremiah was _____ as a
   _____ and _____
   preacher.

5. It will take the _____ of God
   through spirit filled _____.

WEDNESDAY
(Preach with compassion)

1. People in this condition were
   _____ by _____ to be
   _____ to WITH
   _____.

2. It will take a _____ with
   _____ and _____ to
   change them So Preach, **Preach,**
   _____.

3. The _____ between
   _____ and that generation of
   _____ shows the

_____ concerning   fasting
(going without food).

4. *wherefore*[_____]   have   we
   _____ our   soul,   and   thou
   takest _____ knowledge?.."

5. The reasons for _____ and the
   _____ for   doing   so   are
   _____ presented in this chapter.

THURSDAY
(Fast in order to get your prayers answered)

1. Notice   the   _____   reason   for
   _____ is   to   MAKE   YOUR
   PRAYERS _____ ON HIGH
   (verse four).

2. Throughout the Bible in days of great need
   or _____ one will see people
   _____ together, not only to pray
   but   to   _____ **and**
   _____.

3. _____ IN   ORDER   TO   HAVE
   _____ FOR SOUL WINNING
   AND _____

4. "Howbeit   this   _____   goeth
   _____ out but **by prayer and**
   _____."

5. The _____ of _____ and
   _____ is one of the most

Therapy Which Produces Healing

difficult   spiritual _____   for
people to _____ but if there is ever to
be _____ of our nation…IT MUST
BE _____!

FRIDAY
**(God's people must learn to have compassion
as they minister to the poor)**

1. Fasting while _____ God's face in
prayer was _____ by God to
_____ our hearts toward the
_____ of other poor struggling
people.
2. Have _____ as you deal your
bread to the poor – have _____
and help the poor _____ masses
3. Cover   the   _____   of   the
_____ fortunate by _____
them clothes
4. …we should have _____ upon
the hurting and _____ those facilities
and substances to _____ and
_____ the poor.
5. "Then shall thy light _____ forth
as the morning, and thine _____
shall spring forth speedily…"

Daily Declaration

History will repeat itself and America will be destroyed unless we learn a lesson from the destruction of Israel. Honor THE (CHRISTIAN) SABBATH AND KEEP IT HOLY!

.

MY COMMIMMENT

I will strive to become one of those who will fast and pray for the healing of our nation.

Name: _____

Memory Verse

Proverbs 22:6

"Train up a child in the way he should go: and when he is old, he will not depart from it."

	M	T	W	TH	F	S	S
AM							
PM							

- **GIVE YOURSELF AN "A"** if you filled in and reviewed the blanks on a daily basis. This will raise your potential of remembering on an average to 62%
- **GIVE YOURSELF A "B"** if you completed all your blanks before class time.

- **GIVE YOURSELF A "J" FOR JUDGMENT** in order to remind yourself that one has to give account of each day's activity when he takes his finals at the judgment seat of Christ

MY GRADE FOR THIS WEEK IS____

NOTE: Fill in any blanks as you go through the key statement blanks if you have not done so.

LESSON NINE
ABUNDANT HEALTH OR DESTRUCTION

Our lesson is not about life or death. It is about abundant life or total destruction. **It is about absolute healing or total Judgment.**

Jesus came into the world so his children could enjoy more than life (eternal) *John 10:10*. He came that they could enjoy abundant (victorious) life but sadly most of his children draw back to destruction, (*Hebrews 10:39*)(+)

This last practice of spiritual therapy which God has prescribed will lift our nation to the highest plain of abundant living once again; failure will bring destruction.

Fasting and praying becomes easy when it is a matter of life and death.(+) Facing certain death or destruction causing the loss of appetite and triggers a desperate cry to God for help. But it is when the crisis passes and things are running smoothly once again that man has always had a problem.

The final principle of spiritual therapy is the one practice in which the Jews had their greatest problems. This one failure caused the total destruction of their country.(+) Just as God has not changed in his mandate for his people to "observe to do" he has not changed in his absolute demand that the Jews "honor the Sabbath day and keep it holy." It is also just as imperative that God's people remember the Lord's day (Sunday) and keep it holy – If we are going to be healed as a nation.(+) When the Jews honored God's Sabbath day they were blessed. When they forsook the Sabbath day they began to struggle which was followed by their backsliding and destruction.(+) A study of American history will reveal the same pattern.

GOD'S PEOPLE MUST HONOUR
THE LORD'S DAY

Shortly after the Civil War, in the midst of a spiritual awakening, a great preacher, D. L. Moody was saddened almost to the degree of depression, by an event.

The event which saddened the great man of God was the vote of the city Council to allow the trolleys to operate on, as he termed it, the Christian Sabbath (Sunday). Shortly after the vote to use the trolleys on Sunday the church attendance began to drop and the revival fires began to die.

One of the original 10 Commandments was "REMEMBER THE SABBATH DAY, TO KEEP IT HOLY." The 10 Commandments are found in Exodus 20:3-17. These 10 Commandments are recorded in 15 verses. The commentary concerning keeping the Sabbath day occupies four verses. These verses have from 33 1/3 to 40% of the total words found in all the other commandments. God knew that unless people honored the Sabbath day that the other nine Commandments would soon be ignored also.(+)

The death penalty was imposed upon those that did not honor the Sabbath day under the Mosaic law. (Numbers 15:32-36) This shows how serious God is concerning the keeping of the day of worship.

THE PURPOSE OF RESTING ONE DAY

The infinite all-powerful God who created all things not only commanded men to remember the Sabbath day and keep it holy but he demonstrated his command by resting on the seventh day. (Genesis 2:2-3) The word Sabbath means cessation. It was not that God **needed to rest** but wanted to emphasize that man should stop, take time to not only rest his body but to worship God and refresh his soul.

When God made the Sabbath day he hallowed it or made it to be different from any other day. It was the day for man to stop all other activities and focus upon God and His Word. It was a time to teach his children and to rededicate himself anew each Sabbath to God as His Lord. The greatest lesson of resting one day per week was to teach man to REST IN THE LORD; to learn to trust his partner (the Lord) in all things.(+)

THE SABBATH MADE FOR MAN

The religious crowd which confronted Jesus made the **Sabbath day more important than man** who is eternal and was made in the image and likeness of God. They persecuted Jesus because "the Day" became more important than man whom the day was made to benefit. Jesus rebuked them and explained the purpose of the Sabbath when he said unto them,

"... The sabbath **was made for man**, and not man for the sabbath: Therefore the Son of man is **Lord also of the sabbath**." Mark 2:27-28(+)

A WORD OF EXPLANATION ABOUT THE SABBATH DAY

People have gotten a wrong concept concerning the Sabbath day. Their minds have been blinded by the cold, legalistic practice of the Sabbath keepers. When they hear the word, Sabbath, many react negatively because in the past the attitude and spirit of those who espoused that doctrine did so in a cold, non-loving way.

Will you please read about the yearly Sabbath (every seven years) with an open mind and attempt to see the beauty and blessings that a loving father wanted to bestow upon his chosen people? In doing so it may help some of us to have a better understanding of why the Christians of America must have a better understanding and practice of the Lord's day.(+)

THE SABBATH YEAR

God not only commanded His Jewish people to rest every seventh day, but he also implemented a Sabbath year in which the land was to have rest also.(+) That is right; every seventh year was to be a Sabbath year in which the land was to lie idle. The people who tilled and cared for the crops along with the land were to spend the year without cultivating the soil.

GOD'S PLAN FOR ISRAEL

God's plan for Israel was very simple. All it took for the Israelites to succeed was TO HAVE FAITH IN GOD. God did everything in His power to give the Jews basis for trusting Him by;

❖ Miraculously delivering them from the land of Egypt

❖ Miraculously feeding them with manna for 40 years

❖ Miraculously causing the wall of Jericho to fall down

❖ Miraculously placing fear in the hearts of their enemies.

GOD'S REQUIREMENTS FOR THEM TO SUCCEED WERE THREEFOLD

First, drive all the enemies from the land. They failed by compromising. It wasn't until the reign of King David and Solomon several hundred years later that they drove their enemies out of the land.

Second, obey the laws governing the weekly and yearly Sabbath days, which they never did.

Third, Have no idols to worship as gods.

GOD'S PLAN WAS TO DEVELOP A SUPERIOR SOCIETY, A "LAND FLOWING WITH MILK AND HONEY"

Upon complying with His commandments of driving their enemies out of the land, keeping the Sabbath day and worship the one true God; He would be their PARTNER, PROVIDER and their PROTECTOR.(+)

WHAT THE SUPERIOR SOCIETY WOULD MEAN TO GOD

God would be delighted to look down upon a humble generation of obedient people who were looking to him and trusting him for His protection and help.

Every seventh day they would stop all normal activities to worship and learn of Him.(+) Their hearts would be open and their lives would be in compliance with his ordinances.

Every seventh year they would stop all cultivation and let him reenergize the soil. It would be a year long time of praise and thanksgiving to God for giving them abundant crops so they would have sufficient for the year without laboring.

WHAT THE SUPERIOR SOCIETY MEANT TO THE JEWS

The first day of the Sabbath year would be a day of praise and adoration to God. They would exclaim **"Glory to God, I don't have to go to work today!"** (+)

"Nor tomorrow!"

"Nor the next day, or the next week!" This would be the case for an entire year. – Notice some of the blessings:

❖ **Time to rest.** The body gets wore out with pain and aching muscles… I can sleep in. I can rest up. My body can heal itself.

❖ **A Time with the Family.** – I can have time to spend with each of the kids – play games with them. Teach them a special trade – Show them how to do things – Visit my sick, elderly kinfolks.

❖ **Time to repair and do little things;** which one does not have time to do when you go to work at sun-up and work until sundown – a time to beautify our home – our ranch – paint the fences, etc.

❖ **A time for Bible conferences and spiritual awakening.** – To win the gentiles who come see our superior society.

WHAT THE SUPERIOR SOCIETY WOULD MEAN TO THE WORLD

All of the gentile nations surrounding Israel would soon become aware of God's blessings upon their neighbors. They would surely reason:

❖ **We work and slave seven days and we barely exist.** They work for six days and have abundance. It always rains right on time to give them maximum production on

❖ their crops while our crops often time weather in the field.

❖ **They work six days a week for six years and get a full year off.** We work like a dog every day wondering if we will produce enough to feed our families.

❖ **Their houses are painted and well kept.** Their barns are full and picturesque and ours are falling down.

❖ **Their people are healthy** and live years longer than our poor struggling people.

THE RESULTS OF THE JEWISH SUPERIOR SOCIETY

After the Jews "with fear and trembling" tested God and found him to be a faithful provider and protector, their confidence and joy would continually grow.

❖ Their crops produced abundantly. They would praise the Lord for the huge vegetables and fruit which they grew.

❖ Their properties were well kept and beautiful.

❖ Their children were orderly and manifested a godly nature.

❖ They lived in hope of the blessings of the coming Sabbath year.

THEIR FAME TRAVELED ON THE BEAMS OF LIGHT

Within a few years as manifested **in King Solomon's day** people from every land came to see God's blessings upon his nation.

THE RESULTS OF THE SUPERIOR SOCIETY UPON THE WORLD

First the closest neighbors who only had to look across the fence (or in their case, across the valley) to observe the superior society came to see and enquire. Word soon spread until there were multitudes from every part of the world.

❖ **They came to see.** They heard of God's blessings upon the Jewish nation but they couldn't believe the reports. Like the queen of Sheba, after her investigation of Solomon's wisdom and riches went away reporting, "the half has not been told".

❖ **They came to enquire.** "What is your secret?" How do you produce such abundant crops? How do you have such well-kept and beautiful homes and structures? Why are your homes so peaceful and happy and your children so obedient and respectful?" (+)

- ❖ **They came to honour.** They came and brought gifts; thinking it would give them a greater audience.
- ❖ **They came to learn about the Jews great God.** Thousands would accept the Saviour and go home **new creatures.**

This was the main purpose; for God promised blessing upon Israel by giving them a superior society. It was to reveal God's love and goodness and get people to accept the Lord as their Saviour.

ALAS, WHAT A TRAGIC DAY
After all God did for their nation they would not trust him.

- ❖ He Destroyed Egypt for them.
- ❖ He fed them for 40 years (manna)
- ❖ He caused the walls of Jericho to fall and intimidated all of their enemies – But the Jews insulted and rebelled against God through their unbelief.(+)

ALAS, WHAT A TRAGIC
DAY OF JUDGMENT
When God commanded the Jews to let the land rest every 7 years, it was not a suggestion. It

was a command! He meant for the land to rest **every** seventh year.

Israel was in their land for 490 years before God's judgment came. They were carried out of their homeland for 70 years. Seven years divided into 490 years gives you the number of 70 years.(+) The Jews had progressively gotten worse until God judged their rebellion and sin. Read God's inspired account of why he allowed them to be overcome, their home and land destroyed and their survivors carried away as slaves.

"To fulfil the word of the LORD by the mouth of Jeremiah, until the land had enjoyed her sabbaths: *for* as long as she lay desolate she kept sabbath, to fulfil threescore and ten years."

GOD'S WARNINGS CAME TO PASS

When God gave the laws concerning the yearly Sabbaths he spoke of the blessings he would give to them for keeping the Sabbaths in Leviticus 26:3-12. He also sternly warned them of the consequences of their disobedience and rebellion. His exact words are recorded in Leviticus 26:32-36. Please note verse 35, "As long as it [the land] lieth desolate it shall rest; because IT DID NOT REST in your sabbaths, when ye dwelt upon it." Those that were carried out of the land as slaves would suffer "… faintness into their hearts in the lands of their enemies; and the sound of a shaken leaf shall chase them …"(verse 36)

This information was placed in this book by the author for two reasons.

First, to show the intended blessing upon the Jews if only they had "observed to do" as God commanded concerning one day a week to seek after and worship God.(+)

Second, to help you, the reader to have a fuller understanding of why God established a law for his people to hallow and treat as a special day, SO HE COULD BLESS AND PROSPER THEM.(+)

A NEW COMMANDMENT
WITH A NEW DAY

When Jesus fulfilled the Law of Moses by perfectly keeping every ordinance and requirement he took it out of the way, "nailing it to the cross" Colossians 2:14-17. This indicated that the seventh day was NO LONGER COMMANDED to be kept as a special day for worship and instruction about God.

Man's need had not changed, he still needed to stop all activities and honor and worship God.

God's demand had not changed. Man was still to submit to God's ownership and lordship and have one day a week to rest his body and refresh his mind and spirit. The Mosaic Law was to serve as a schoolmaster, which pointed men to a better way of life as they served Christ. It did not lower the requirements of what God expected of man but it clarified why man should surrender his all to Jesus as his Lord. His command to men is very clear. They are to reach a lost world with the gospel.

ONLY THE DAY WAS CHANGED

The Jews kept the seventh day and hallowed it. The Jewish law expected and commanded Israel to do so but the Gentiles (the majority of the world) **was never under the law of Moses** as their rule of faith and practice.

Upon the resurrection of Jesus the day to stop, rest, learn and teach about Jesus was changed. It was changed from the seventh day to the first day of the week in order to remember and commemorate THE RESURRECTION OF JESUS FROM THE DEAD.

Creating the world cost God **a little effort** but the redemption of fallen man **COST GOD HIS SON**. When Jesus appeared several times to the disciples before ascending back to heaven it was it was upon the first day of the week.

The disciples **were to meet upon the first day** of the week **every first day of the week** to worship and praise God for giving His life as a perfect Saviour on the cross. He proved He was holy by taking up His life on the first day of the week. (Romans 1:4) That day became the most important day that the world ever witnessed. Man's creator and maintainer had died and now OCCUPIED THE POSITION OF THEIR REDEEMER. He arose the first day of the week. Ever since then people have gathered on that special day to celebrate their redemption and to worship God. They are to stop and honor God as the Lord **for the whole day**. The token appearance in church for a few minutes on the Lord's day is not pleasing to God. The day was made for man's benefit and will improve every thing in mans life if he uses THE WHOLE DAY to rest his body and refresh his soul as he honors God on the Lord's day. Notice the following statements concerning the Lords Sabbath:

- **Call the Sabbath day (Lord's Day) a delight**
  You are growing spiritually when you reach the level that you love to go to God's house. Going to church to worship the Lord becomes A DELIGHT INSTEAD OF A DUTY.

- **The Holy of the Lord** - You are growing in grace and becoming more like the Lord because the day God has set aside to bless and refresh His people has been given its proper place, **the holy of the Lord**.

- **You call the Lord's Day Honorable** - The Lord's day is no longer just like any other day. It is special.(+) It is the day that **the whole family looks forward to and enjoys.**

- **And shall honour HIM** - It is His day that we take our family to His house and honour Him. We honour His word by "observing to do", we honour His ownership by worshiping with our "tithes and offerings" **and strive to get sinners saved**.

HEALING OF AMERICA IS CONTINGENT UPON HONORING THE LORD'S DAY

The unchangeable God has not changed! Man's needs to become a spiritual, godly person has not changed. God saw that it would take one day each week for man to set aside as a special day to live the type of life which God could honor and bless. This truth is an important fact for the people of America to understand and practice.

They must return again to this practice in order for God to heal our nation.(+)

Isaiah 58:13 set down their requirements to obtain healing and a close relationship with the Lord. God promises that obeying the requirements in verse (13) would bring indescribable blessings, and close fellowship with Christ in this life as well as eternal rewards. Let us analyze that important verse:

"If thou turn away thy foot from the sabbath, from doing thy pleasure on my holy day; and call the sabbath a delight, the holy of the LORD, honourable; and shalt honour him, not doing thine own ways, nor finding thine own pleasure, nor speaking thine own words:"

PLEASE NOTE THE CORRECTIONS ONE MUST MEET IN ORDER TO OBTAIN THESE GREAT BLESSINGS.

The statement, **"turn away thy foot from the Sabbath"** means instead of going to church and worshiping God as commanded one goes and seeks his own pleasure.

Later in the same verse the Holy Spirit deals with the things one must stop doing on the Lord's day. Please note the three actions people must stop doing on the Lord's day in order to receive God's FULL BLESSINGS:

- **Not doing my own ways**; working, fishing, or following one's hobby on the Lord's day
- **Finding thine own pleasure means** living for your own self gratification on the Lord's day.
- **Speaking thy own words.** This means stop furthering your own cause because you have six days to do that.

In the middle of the verse it gives the right attitude toward the Lord's Day. The proper attitude toward the Lord's Day is summed up in the statement CALL THE SABBATH A DELIGHT.

The expression reveals that the heart is right with the Lord. Sunday becomes the most enjoyable day of the week. Sunday is the day that all the family loves and looks forward to; A DELIGHT!(+)

THE DAY FOCUSES AROUND GOD, HIS HOUSE, ALONG WITH FAMILY AND FRIENDS

Please note how God emphasizes His point concerning His special day. He gives the things people are not to do on his special day and then states the proper attitude toward His day.

- **The holy of the Lord** - Please note the expression, the Holy of the Lord. It is THE Holy, **not "a" holy of the Lord**. Everything done on that day points TO HIM.

- **Honorable** - **The day is respected as honorable**. A person is proud to be a Christian and considers it to be an honor to be able to serve God. The negative feedback from friends, family and the world is not a hardship but it is a joy. It becomes an honor to be able to have God's peace, even if there is opposition to God which is directed toward the person.

- **And shall honour Him**. It is all about Him. He died for us, He hears our prayers, He cares and protects us. He is the hope of curing America and it is an honour to serve Him **with our praise, our finances and with our all!**

His promise of HEALING (verse 8).
His promise of REBUILDING AND OVERCOMING APOSTASY (verse 12)

His promise of riding upon the high places of the earth for 1000 years with Jesus, as king (verse 14) **are immutable promises.** BUT THOSE PROMISES ARE ALSO CONDITIONAL.

These promises are based upon God's people performing THEIR SPIRITUAL THERAPY.(+)

- **Preachers must preach**
- **People must fast and pray**
- **People must honor the Lord's Day in order to be able to constantly perform these spiritual therapies daily**

The God who wanted to heal the past generation of sick societies wants to heal America. HIS IMMUTABLE PROMISES ARE SURE! His love for sinners is great and if enough people in our generation will believe his promise and meet his conditions then revival and healing will return to America.(+)

POINTS TO PONDER

❖ God, in order to bless Israel, instituted The Sabbath Principles

❖ Israel failed to understand God's purpose and blessings

❖ Israel drew back in unbelief to their destruction

❖ God is the same God and longs to bless America

❖ Sunday is the Lord's day in commemoration of Jesus resurrection

❖ Honoring the Lord's Day brings God's blessings

❖ Dishonoring the Lord's Day will bring total destruction

MONDAY
(Abundant Health or Destruction)

1. He came that they could enjoy _____ (victorious) life but _____ most of his children _____ back to , (*Hebrews 10:39*)
2. Fasting and _____ becomes _____ when it is a matter of _____ and _____.
3. This one _____ caused the total _____ of their country.
4. It is also just as _____ that God's people remember the _____ day (Sunday) and keep it _____ – If we are going to be _____ as a nation.
5. When they forsook the Sabbath day they began to struggle which was followed by their backsliding and destruction.

TUESDAY
(God's people must honour the Lord's day)

1. One of the original 10 Commandments was "_____ THE SABBATH DAY, TO KEEP IT _____."
2. God knew that unless people _____ the Sabbath day that the _____ other nine Commandments

would _____ be _____
also.

3. The greatest _____ of resting one
day per week was to reach man to
_____ IN THE LORD; to learn to
trust his partner (the Lord) in _____
things.

4. "...The Sabbath **was** _____ **for**
_____, and not _____ for the
Sabbath: Therefore the Son of man is **Lord
also of the Sabbath.**"

5. In doing so it may help some of us to have
a better _____ of why the
Christians of America _____ have a
_____ understanding and
_____ of the _____ day.

WEDNESDAY
(The Sabbath year)

1. God not _____ commanded His
Jewish people to rest every
_____ day, but he also
implemented a _____ year in
which the land was to have _____
also.

2. He would be their _____,
PROVIDER and their PROTECTOR.

3. They would exclaim "_____ **to God, I don't have to** _____ **to work** _____!"

4. Every _____ day they would stop all _____ activities to _____ and _____ of Him.

5. Why are your _____ so peaceful and _____ and your _____ so obedient and _____?"

THURSDAY
(Alas, what a tragic day)

1. But the Jews _____ and _____ against God through their _____.

2. _____ years divided into _____ years gives you the number of _____ years.

3. Those that were _____ out of the land as _____ would suffer "..._____ into their _____ in the lands of their _____; and the sound of a shaken leaf shall chase them..."

4. **First,** to show the intended _____ upon the Jews _____ only they had "_____ to do" as God _____ concerning _____

day a week to seek after and _____ God.

5. **Second,** to help you, the reader to have a fuller _____ of why God established a law for his people to _____ and treat as a _____ day, SO HE COULD _____ AND _____ THEM.

FRIDAY
(A New Commandment with a new day)

1. The _____ day is no longer just like any other _____. It is _____.

2. They must return again to this _____ in order for God to _____ our _____.

3. Sunday is the day that _____ the family _____ and _____ forward to; A _____!

4. These _____ and _____ upon God's people _____ THEIR SPIRITUAL THERAPY.

5. His _____ for sinners is great and if _____ people in our generation will _____ his _____ and _____ his conditions then revival and _____ will return to America.

Daily declaration

Powerful, Spirit filled preaching depends on the prayer and fasting of God's people as they cry out for revival.

MY COMMIMMENT

I will incorporate periods of fasting and praying into my life for the healing of our Nation.

Name: _____

Memory Verse

ISAIAH 58:8

Then shall thy light break forth as the morning, **and thine health shall spring forth speedily**: and thy righteousness shall go before thee; the glory of the LORD shall be thy rereward..

	M	T	W	TH	F	S	S
AM							
PM							

LESSON TEN
VOLUNTEER TO BECOME A DOCTOR

There is a great need for volunteers to work in God's nursery.(+) Please review our questions and deductions in order to determine God's will and solution in healing our nation.

IS OUR ANALYSIS CORRECT?

Please check and consider the analysis of our nation's condition along with the court case histories we have studied.

WERE THE GENERATION'S SICK?

First, does the United States of America have the symptoms of a sick society?(+)

Second, did the griping, complaining, rebellious nation of Israel in Moses' day resemble anything close to a godly nation?(+)

Third, were the practices of the Jewish nation, as presented in the book of Judges, holy or that of a sick nation?(+)

Fourth, with all of the pagan temples, not one place for the worship of God, and no book of the Law, was Josiah born into a sick society?

Fifth, was the apostle Paul abandoned by a sick society?(+)

Volunteer to Become a Doctor

WERE THERE LESSONS TO BE LEARNED FROM EACH CASE HISTORY?

First, what were the lessons learned from the apostasy in Moses' day?

The answer was: They were still under the mandate to (observe to do) God's command.(+)

Second, what were the lessons learned from the apostasies in the book of Judges?

THE LESSONS LEARNED WERE:

- God would take drastic action to cure an apostasy.(+)
- Apostasies would occur over and over again.(+)
- After the days of apostasy, God could build a high level of moral life and national glory. (+)

Third, what were the lessons learned from the apostasy, which had degenerated into complete pagan worship as found in Josiah's day?

THE LESSONS LEARNED WERE:

- God will use anyone who loves him with all of his heart, soul and might to bring revival.

- God can still send revival to a generation that is so sinful that he has already appointed a day of destruction.(+)

DURING THE LIFE OF PAUL, WHAT WERE THE LESSONS LEARNED IN THE FIRST GREAT APOSTASY IN THE CHURCH ERA?

God allowed a great falling away from Paul's ministry. This devastated Paul. God then comforted Paul and taught him how to comfort other pastors during their heartbreak caused by apostasy.

Paul gave Timothy assurance that the men who had caused the apostasy in Moses' day were overcome by the practice of God's Word. He explained to Timothy that following the same principles would overcome Timothy's dark days.

The Bible will completely furnish unto all good works, including the good works of how to overcome a falling away. In it, God gave four simple principles which would overcome any dark day of apostasy if they were only followed.(+)

GOD'S ANTIDOTE TO CURE APOSTASY

After Paul went over the conditions which prevailed in any apostasy in His second letter to Timothy He gave four principles **which were**

simply stated. The simplicity of these four principles have been hidden from a generation whose eyes have been blinded by tradition. Many in this generation either do not believe there is any hope for national revival or are to busy following traditional "church work" to examine its possibility.

Consider these four simple steps, which will overcome our apostasy. These four principles cannot be stated any clearer or penned more briefly than when they were first stated in II Timothy 4:5, they are:

First	Watch in all things
Second	Endure afflictions
Third	Do the work of an evangelist
Fourth	Make full proof of the ministry

WERE THE PRINCIPLES, WHICH CAUSED OUR DAY OF APOSTASY EXPLAINED CLEARLY?

THE PRINCIPLES AND PRACTICES, AS CLEARLY DEFINED OR IMPLIED, WHICH CAUSED OUR APOSTASY, WERE:

- The expulsion of the Bible, prayer, and patriotism from schools **produced a bitter**, rebellious, and anti-Christian spirit in many.(+)

- Humanism, socialism, and welfare programs destroyed the initiative and character of many who no longer have the will to live moral or holy lives.

- The desire for the "American dream" instead of the "heavenly vision" has caused many of our generation to stress the secular life, **and live like there was no eternal.**

- The stress on individual rights has led to a spirit of self-centeredness and a desire to be served instead of the spirit of the Bible, which is to become a servant.

- The acceptance of the world's definition of a Christian, **"to go to the church of your choice on Sunday morning,"** instead of the Bible's definition of a Christian has led to the abandonment of local churches for the mega-churches where they sit and listen.

- In the zeal of gospel preaching churches to save people from hell, they did not properly follow-up and stabilize their converts which caused the loss of a whole generation of practicing Christians.

- In the zeal of gospel preaching to save people from hell, churches did not inform them of the twofold nature of the child of

God. The new converts continued to feed the flesh and were soon overcome by sinful habits and fell back into their old life, disenchanted with Christianity.(+)

- Many of our finest Christians have bought into the philosophy that "**they have earned the right to retire**" and have abandoned their positions of responsibility in local churches in order to travel.
- The breakdown of role models **in the political, entertainment, athletic, and religious worlds** has left the American people in a state of mind, which makes it easy for them to believe the negative preaching in many churches. They have **developed an almost fatal case of the "last day blues".**

These problems and practices have been the major contributors to the horrible apostasy, which is destroying our nation. But there is good news and hope in our faith building OPERATIONAL MANUAL, THE BIBLE.

WERE THE SOLUTIONS FOR OVERCOMING THE PROBLEMS IN OUR SICK SOCIETY LOGICAL?

The solutions in every case history were the same. They can be summed up in the following words, **observe to do God's Word.**

In order to raise a new generation of Christians, we must return to the mandate of the great commission which is, **as ye go, make men into disciples**. In order to stress the literalness and the spirit of this mandate, we will stress it in a more revealing way, **as ye go, make BABIES INTO DISCIPLES**.

Some simple comparisons in raising domestic babies and spiritual babies were made in order to help us understand our personal responsibility.

Discipling people into good healthy people MUST start as soon as they are saved. You MUST place a spiritual role model over each new convert in order to keep him from **learning bad habits from nominal Christians, friends, and family members** who profess to be Christians.(+) We must break our traditional habits of dealing with people **in an impersonal way,** and realize that the only way to raise a new generation is TO PROTECT, PACIFY, AND DEVELOP OUR BABIES. Then we can bring change and healing to our nation.

As we work in our tasks to be obedient to our blessed Saviour who gave us life by giving His life, we must remember two things:

- The judgment hand of God can only be stayed from falling upon our beloved nation **if we repent** of our slothfulness and raise a new generation of healthy children.(+)
- The judgment hand of God can only be stayed if we will begin to follow a rigor plan of spiritual exercises as outlined in God's word which was presented in lesson eight.

AN ETERNAL LINE AND A TINY DOT

There is a story of a pastor of a large church who created a real stir in his complacent congregation. There were even threats of his dismissal for disfiguring God's **"holy property"**. They even reported him to his state superintendent.

What did this godly old pastor do that was so awful? How did he disfigure God's "holy property"? He drew a black line from the left side of the rear of the auditorium down the whole side of the huge auditorium, and then across the front, and back to the rear on the opposite wall.

He even drew a line across **all of the stained-glass windows**.

What was the purpose for this unusual, and as some called it, **"eccentric behavior"**? Each service he would go to a different spot in the auditorium and make a tiny dot with his fine tipped pen.

STRANGE INDEED!

Then he would preach the same sermon each service. This went on service after service for several weeks.

What was the message of this determined pastor who caused such a storm of protest as he labored to make his "POINT"?

He would explain that the line, which he had drawn all around the huge auditorium, stood FOR ETERNITY. The line will never end, just as eternity will never end.(+)

Each week he would walk around the auditorium as he emphasized that eternity would never end for those in…**HELL**!

He would say that the little dot represented the life of people who lived in time, died, and went to hell!

...THEIR SUFFERING WOULD
NEVER END…(+)

He would walk the length of the huge auditorium, from one corner to the front, then across the front to the left corner, preaching about the brevity of life in contrast to **the endlessness of eternity**. He would always **stop**...take out his fine tip pen, and make a single dot on the line, which represented the endlessness of eternity ...

HIS POINT!

This tiny dot, which you could not even see, represented your life—the life you **so carefully try to preserve and continue.(+)**

The next service would be almost exactly like the last service. He would walk the auditorium and preach saying, "This line represents the endlessness of eternity, and will never end for those in...HEAVEN!"

He would take a fine tip pen and place a dot on the wall. Sometimes he would say, "YOUR LIFE IS LIKE A VAPOR... The sun comes up and your life is GONE!"

Next service he would place another dot with his fine tip pen and preach about the endlessness of eternity. He would say, "The Bible describes YOUR LIFE LIKE A STORY THAT HAS BEEN TOLD."

The next week he would walk and point to the line, which represented **the endlessness of eternity**. He would place a dot with his fine tip pen and say, "YOUR LIFE IS LIKE 'A PUFF OF SMOKE'."(+)

Next service, as he placed the dot with a fine tip pen, he would say, "YOUR LIFE IS LIKE

LAST NIGHT'S SLEEP". On and on he went, service after service.

YOUR LIFE IS LIKE...a watch in the night (a brief three hours period).

Next service he would follow the long line around the huge auditorium, stop, make a dot, and say: "YOUR LIFE IS LIKE FLOWERS, which bloom, they fade or are soon cut down."

Then a strange thing began to happen...**The criticism stopped**...THE CROWD GREW...PEOPLE BEGAN TO BE SAVED. Some surrendered to special service as missionaries. Then, **the old preacher's life ended and his little dot (life) passed into the endlessness of eternity.(+)** His death was like a big AMEN from God. The old preacher no longer walks and preaches, but his message still lives on in the lives of many.

YOUR ABSOLUTE GUARANTEE

Please take a few minutes and give prayerful thought about WHAT YOU POSSESS AND WHO YOU ARE. **The gift of God is eternal life.** That is the endless life the old preacher was preaching about.

The Bible declares, **"For God so loved the world [mankind], that he gave his only begotten Son, that whosoever believeth in him (Jesus), should not perish, BUT HAVE**

EVERLASTING LIFE. [ETERNAL LIFE]"
John 3:16

Paul preached, "the gift of God is **eternal life** through Jesus Christ our Lord." Romans 6: 23

John stated, "Beloved, now are we **the sons of God**, and it does not yet appear what we shall be: but we know that, when he shall appear, WE SHALL BE LIKE HIM; for we shall see him as he is." I John 3:2

John tells us that eternal life is in Jesus, **"And this is the record, that God hath <u>given to us eternal life</u>, and this life is in his Son. He that hath the Son hath life; and he that hath not the Son of God hath not life. These things have I written unto you that believe on the name of the Son of God, that ye may <u>know that ye have eternal life</u>, and that ye may believe on the name of the Son of God."** I John 5:11-13

John further explained as he said, **"He came unto his own (Jewish people), and his own received him not. But as many as received him, to them gave he power to become <u>the sons of God</u>, even them that believe on his name: Which were born, not of blood, nor of the will of the flesh, nor of the will of man, but of God."** John 1:11-13

BEFORE GOING TO HEAVEN, JESUS PROMISED HIS CHILDREN A MANSION

"In my Father's house are many mansions: if it were not so, I would have told you. I go to prepare a place for you. And if I go and prepare a place for you, I will come again, and receive you unto myself; that where I am, there ye may be also." John 14:2-3

PAUL TALKED ABOUT A PARADISE.

He said, "How that he (Paul) was caught up INTO PARADISE." II Corinthians 12:4

PAUL TEACHES THAT THOSE WHO ARE SAVED ARE AS GOOD AS IN HEAVEN NOW.

In Romans 8:30, he states, "Moreover whom he did predestinate, them he also <u>called</u>: and whom he <u>called</u>, [past tense] them he also <u>justified</u>: (past tense) and whom he <u>justified</u>, them he also <u>glorified</u>." [past tense]

In Romans 8:28, Paul had already stated, "And we know that all things work together for good to them that love God, to them who are the called according to his purpose."

Add all of these promises up!!

What do all these promises mean?

❖ **First**, the child of God has eternal life.
❖ **Second**, the child of God has a mansion reserved in heaven.

❖ **Third**, the child of God is already **a son** of God

❖ **Fourth**, the child of God will receive a glorified body like the body of Jesus.

❖ **Fifth**, God's child will live in a **perfect paradise as a member of God's royal family forever**.(+)

❖ **Sixth**, the child of God, in the mind and eyes of the Lord, is as good **as in heaven this very minute**. Notice once again the words, **called**, **justified**, and **glorified**.

- **Called** by the Holy Spirit through the preaching of the Gospel.

- **Justified** by faith through the shed blood of Jesus.

- **Glorified**, just as though the rapture had already happened and we were in our glorified bodies in heaven.

You are a possessor of eternal life. You have a title deed to a mansion. It is yours, just as if you were sitting in your living room in heaven RIGHT NOW.

YOU ARE A MEMBER OF THE ROYAL FAMILY, A CHILD OF GOD

You are as good as being thrilled with the sights of heaven as if you were there this very minute. Visualize yourself walking on the streets of gold and basking in the love of God now! In God's mind you are as good as in heaven right now. You have the ABSOLUTE PROMISE of God that it is yours as if you had already moved into your eternal mansion.

I AM GOING TO ASK YOU TO MAKE A DECISION. We are coming to the close of this book on God's CURE FOR OUR NATION. We began by saying the doctor had diagnosed a plan of healing for the patient, **IF, AND ONLY IF,** the patient would strictly follow His therapy.

If there is hope for our survival as a nation, we, the citizens of the United States, are the ones who must follow the instructions in OUR LIFE'S MANUAL.

Before you make your decision, please consider some important truths:

❖   God gave you your life.

❖   God gave you life to glorify and give him pleasure. (Revelation 4:11)

❖   God maintains your life, **"in him we live, and move, and have our being;"** Acts 17:28

❖   God will send his Son soon; time is short.

❖   We must all appear before Christ at the judgment seat to give account of our deeds.

❖ People will suffer forever in hell unless they are saved.

❖ Jesus gave His life on the cross to save us (sinners).

❖ God gave you life in order to lead sinners to Jesus for salvation.

❖ You have eternal life and are as sure of living in paradise in a glorified body as if you were already there.

Now look at the line which represents ETERNAL LIFE, which stretches from eternity past, through the course of your life, and on into the endlessness of the ages to come. Look at the tiny dot that represents your life; it will soon be passed!(+) You can not keep it. It is fleeing rapidly away...

Now, BECOME THE MOST CHRIST-LIKE PERSON YOU CAN and imitate Jesus by giving your life away. Do this so that others (masses) can escape the horrors of hell and **live with you** in God's paradise as the endlessness of the line continues on and on forever.

Do this by...VOLUNTEERING TO BECOME A DOCTOR. Work in the Lord's nursery by developing an army of healthy babies who will grow and restore health to our nation.(+)

POINTS TO PONDER

❖ There is hope for healing **for our sick nation.**

❖ God is looking for servants who will develop healthy new converts.

❖ God's ways are clearly defined…

❖ God's promises are immutable…

❖ God is waiting for your complete surrender

❖ He has promised to "heal speedily"…

❖ It will be **healing** or DESTRUCTION…

REMEMBER…
Your only life will soon be passed…
[see the little • (dot) which
represents your life]
ONLY WHAT IS DONE FOR JESUS
WILL LAST.

Volunteer to Become a Doctor

MONDAY
(Volunteer to Become a Doctor)

1. There is a _____ need for _____ to work in _____ nursery.
2. Does the United _____ have the _____ of a _____society?
3. Did the _____, complaining, rebellious nation of _____ in Moses' day _____ anything close to a _____ nation?
4. Were the _____ of the Jewish nation in the book of Judges _____ or that of a _____ nation?
5. Was the apostle Paul _____ by a _____ society?

TUESDAY
(Were There Lessons to be Learned?)

1. They were _____ under the mandate to (_____ to do) God's commands.
2. God would take _____ action to _____ an apostasy.
3. Apostasies would occur _____ and _____ again.

4.   After the days of _____, God would _____ a high level of _____ life and national _____.

5.   God can _____ send revival to a generation that he has already _____ to a _____ of destruction.

WEDNESDAY
(What is the Lesson Learned in the First Apostasy?)

1.   God gave _____ simple principles, which would _____ any dark day of apostasy.

2.   The _____ of the Bible, _____, and _____ from schools produced a _____, rebellious, and _____ spirit in many.

3.   The new converts _____ to _____ the flesh and were soon _____ by sinful habits and _____ back into their old life.

4.   You _____ place a _____ role model over _____ new convert to keep him from _____ bad habits from _____ Christians.

5. The judgment _____ of God can only be _____ if we repent of our _____ and raise a _____ generation of _____ children.

THURSDAY
(An Eternal Line and A Tiny Dot)

1. The line _____ never _____ just as eternity _____ never end.
2. He would say, their _____ will _____ end."
3. This _____ dot you cannot even_____ … represents your life… the life you so _____ try to _____ and continue.
4. "Your _____ is like a _____ of smoke"
5. Then the old _____ life ended and his _____(like) passed into the _____ of eternity.

FRIDAY
(Your Absolute Guarantee)

1. Paul teaches that those who _____ saved are as _____ as in heaven now.

2.   A child of God will _____ in a perfect _____ as a _____ of God's royal _____ forever.

3.   Look at the _____ dot which represents your _____ it will _____ be passed.

4.   Become the most _____ person you can and _____ Jesus by giving your _____ away so that _____ can escape the _____ of hell and _____ in paradise with you as the _____ of the line continues.

5.   Volunteer to become a _____ and work in the _____ nursery.

Daily Declaration

God gave me life and continues my life day by day in order for me to give my life back to him.

Memory Verse

II Corinthians 5:15

And that He died for all, that they which live should not henceforth live unto them-selves, but unto him which died for them, and rose again.

	M	T	W	TH	F	S	S
AM							
PM							

Books By the Author

These booklets and books are presented to help the laymen in the local church. We are dedicated to aiding the Pastor in strengthening members through the New Convert Care Discipleship Program, we help new converts become happy, active parts of the church family.

Through the Layman Library Series, we present books designed to train and strengthen. Please contact the author for prices.

* Denote Discipleship materials

THE LAYMAN LIBRARY SERIES

100   * A Letter to a New Convert
102   How to Have Something in Heaven When You Get There
105   Incentives in Soul-winning
106   How to Pray So God Will Answer You
111   Points and Poems by Pearl – Pearl Cheeves
112   Foreknowledge in The Light of Soul-winning
113   Elected "To Go"
114   Predestination Promotes Soul-winning
115   The Ministry of Paul in the Light of Soul-winning
116   The Church, a Place of Protection, Love & Development

OTHER BOOKS BY DR. WILKINS

Foreknowledge, Election, & Predestination in the Light Of Soul-winning(160p)
Essentials to Successful Soul-Winning (258p)
Designed to Win (Soul winning Manuel) (120p)
Harvest Time(110p)
*Milk of The Word – (Book One) (also in Spanish) (146p)
*From Salvation to Service (also in Spanish) (40p)
*How to Be a Better Big Brother (40p)
*Big Brother Bits (40p)
*Questions Concerning Baptism (40p)
*Four Tremendous Truths (61p)
*The Mission of The Church (Not Available) (198p)
Healing Words for Lonely People
How To Raise A King (64p)
*Healing Words for Hurting people (120p)
Thy Kingdom Come (46p)
The Truth About Hell (101p)
The Kindergarten Phase of Eternity (170p)
The Final Flight (50p)
The Short Race Home (50p)
Not Even a Nickel, Just A Penny (Testimony of Penny Wilkins)(40p)
A Struggle to Peace (Cindy Benson) (58p)
*The Meat of The Word (186p)
God's Cure for America
God's Brilliant Plan to Reach Fallen Man

Dr. James Wilkins, Director
New Testament Ministries

56 Arroyo Seco Circle
Espanola, NM 85732
505-747-6917
E-Mail
penny@jameswilkins.org
leatherman_wave@yahoo.com

RANGER BEAR

RANGER BEAR: RILEY

SILVERTIP SHIFTERS

J.K. HARPER